Catching
THE PLAYER

the hamilton family series

Diane Alberts

Entangled Publishing, LLC
2614 South Timberline Road
Suite 109
Fort Collins, CO 80525
Visit our website at www.entangledpublishing.com.

Indulgence is an imprint of Entangled Publishing, LLC.

Edited by Candace Havens
Cover design by Erin Dameron-Hill
Cover art from iStock

Manufactured in the United States of America

First Edition October 2017

This one goes out to my daughter, Kaitlyn. I'm so proud of you and all you've accomplished. One day, you'll find the kind of love I write books about, and you'll know that all the pain, and all the wrong turns along the way, were all just your way of finding your happily ever after.

Chapter One

He couldn't be serious. He couldn't possibly be asking her to do this. No way. No how. Not even her brother would stoop that low...would he?

"Absolutely not," Kassidy Thomas said, shaking her head for good measure. "I'm not wearing that or doing that. Are you crazy?"

Caleb, her annoying older brother who acted like he was still thirteen instead of thirty, waved the offensive item under her nose, clearly refusing to take no for an answer. Like usual. "You have to do it. A deal's a deal."

She crossed her arms, frowning, and shook her head again. There was no way in hell she was doing what he wanted. No. Way. "You had insider information. Admit it."

"How the hell would I have had inside information on the condition of Wyatt Hamilton's arm? Come on." He shoved the green contraption under her nose again. Kassidy was *this close* to punching him in the stomach like she had when they were in high school and he'd told every boy he knew she was a lesbian so none of them would ask her to prom. "Stop being such a sore loser."

Stiffening, she uncrossed her arms and shoved her glasses into place, reminding herself calmly that she was an adult now, and punching people was not an acceptable response to annoyance...no matter how big a jerk her brother could be. "I'm not a sore loser."

"Then put on the outfit, and stop pouting." He wiggled it again, way too excited at her impending embarrassment. "It's just one song you have to deliver to some stranger, and you'll never see them again. A couple of minutes. No big deal."

"Who is it being delivered to? Man, or woman?"

"It doesn't say," he glanced at the paper, frowning. "A dude ordered it, though, so probably a woman."

Well, at least there was *that*.

"You've heard me sing before," she muttered, her cheeks hot. She scrambled for the papers on her desk and held them up, pointing to them angrily. "There's a reason I do numbers and stay in here. I don't have an artistic bone in my body. My singing is even worse."

That was the truth. Ever since the third grade, she'd been pretty much banned from all musicals in her school, and her mother had forbidden her from singing anywhere but in the shower—with the door closed. Some might call it cruel, but Kassidy considered it necessary honesty. Hey, if you sucked at something, you *sucked* at something.

It was your parents' job to tell you as much.

Caleb laughed. "That's the best part. The client requested 'For he's a Jolly Good Fellow' and wants you to dress in a fairytale costume—though, I'm not sure how the two go together, to be honest. But either way, Dad got this costume and didn't realize it was woman's, so it might be the only chance this little guy gets to see the light of day."

She slammed her papers down on the desk. "You're seriously going to make me do this?"

"I'm seriously gonna make you do this." He focused on Kassidy, not breaking eye contact. He had hair the same shade of blond as hers, and a dimple in his chin. He'd always been a prankster, but this took it too far. "Besides, weren't you just saying you wanted to try being a little more adventurous and a little less safe?"

"I meant by going hiking, or taking a painting class." She came around the side of the desk. "Not making a fool out of myself in front of some stranger."

"Better that than someone you know."

Well, he had a point there. But *still*. "This is all Wyatt Hamilton's fault," she muttered.

"It's not his fault his arm healed better than anticipated," Caleb said, grinning. "Comes with being a beast on and off the field."

Yeah, from what she'd heard, he definitely fit that description. The star quarterback from the Atlanta Saviors was never alone, and never seen with the same woman twice. He had quite the reputation as a "beast" and certainly didn't seem to mind it.

Rolling her eyes, she snatched the outfit out of his hand. It was ridiculously green and ugly. She'd never make a good Peter Pan, or Tinkerbelle, or whatever the heck this was supposed to be. Wyatt Hamilton had been injured last month, and the rumor had been that he would be out of the game for the rest of the regular season. With their best player out, Kassidy has been sure that they would lose to the Pelicans for the first time ever. Caleb bet they'd win as always, and she'd taken that bet. Then Hamilton, jerk that he was, had healed quickly and rejoined the game.

Hence the situation she was now in.

"Don't forget the tiara thing on the hanger," Caleb said, grinning way too widely.

She clenched her teeth. "I'll shove that tiara right up your ass—"

"*Kassidy!*" her father admonished, walking down the hallway with a bouquet of flowers in his hand. "Language."

Her cheeks heated, and she called out, "Sorry, Dad."

He lifted a hand and kept walking.

Caleb laughed.

She pushed him out of her office and slammed the door shut. Trembling, she fought the urge to kick the door for good measure. He always one-upped her. She should never have taken that stupid bet. If he'd told her this was the price she would have to pay, she wouldn't have.

No way.

Though, he was right about one thing. At their annual Octoberfest dinner a couple of weeks ago, she lamented that she'd spent most of her twenty-six years acting like she was in a bubble, refusing to actually live. She'd been tipsy at the time, sure, but it was the truth, even so.

She didn't take risks.

Didn't date.

Didn't ever jump into anything with both feet.

She overthought everything and lost the only man she ever loved because of it. Her high school sweetheart had gone to the same college as her. They'd made plans to move in together after they graduated, and had talked about marriage—though, she had been undecided on the number of kids she wanted, if any. She'd also been unable to commit to their wedding date, venue, size and, really, to whether or not they should get married at all.

She'd loved Jake with all her heart, and she'd thought he loved her, too, until he left her the week before graduation for some girl named Debbie with big boobs and even bigger hair. He'd told her that her indecisiveness had driven him mad and that if she could ever learn to make up her mind about a single thing without overthinking it, then maybe he'd think about taking her back.

Well, she'd made up her mind all right—she didn't want Jake back, and she'd decided not to date anymore because men were the devil incarnate.

That had been four years ago.

Four. Years.

At the time, giving up on men seemed right, and backing down from her decision had been too reminiscent of indecision (something she'd just been left for), so for better or worse...she'd stuck to it. In the process, she also stopped doing anything else exciting, and though she'd been alive, she hadn't really lived in years.

It was sobering.

Her admission was probably why Caleb chose this particular brand of payback, but he was missing the point. She wanted to *live*, not make a fool of herself. Then again, wasn't that a part of living? Making mistakes and being able to recover from them?

Sighing, she locked the door and undressed.

As she slid into the tights that her brother had asked her to wear, she sucked in a breath and yanked them up. They were practically a second layer of skin and would leave nothing to the imagination. Literally *nothing*.

Breathing shallowly in case she tore them, she glanced around her office in her parents' flower shop, which was another reminder that she'd always chosen the safe route as opposed to the road less traveled. When she was a child, she'd wanted to be an author, but the second she realized that it was an uncertain job with unrealistic salary expectations, she'd instead opted to become an accountant and after graduation had taken over management of her parents' shop.

Under her management, Thomas Flowers was booming, and for the first time ever, they were showing a bigger profit than when they'd first opened in 2001. It had been her idea to add singing telegrams to the menu of things offered, a decision she wholly regretted right now, thank you very much.

She slid the top over her head and tugged on it until it covered her stomach. It was even tighter than the pants, if that was possible. When she glanced down, her eyes bugged out because *holy frigging cleavage.* She cupped her breasts, laughing uneasily. She always wore sensible necklines and never let her boobs hang out, but then again, they'd never looked like *this.*

Maybe she'd been wearing the wrong clothes all this time.

"Thank you, corsets," she muttered, turning and checking out her ass, too. "*Whoa.*"

Then she smiled because when Caleb saw her in this outfit, he was going to have a heart attack. He'd always been an overprotective brother, so this would kill him. Maybe it made her petty to want her revenge, but whatever.

At least she'd be petty with some amazing boobs.

After sliding into the skirt, she took her hair out of its usual bun and fluffed it with her fingers, hoping it went with what *had* to be a sexy Halloween costume that teenaged girls wore to get laid by some hot college boys. Not that she knew what that was like. She'd only ever had sex with her ex, and it hadn't been that exciting. In her opinion, she hadn't been missing much in that department while she'd put her life on hold.

In fact, she didn't miss it at all.

"Maybe sex has gotten better these past four years," she muttered. After one last glance at her cleavage, she opened the door and came walking out. "Okay, off I go."

Caleb's reaction was immediate. "What the *hell* is that?"

"What?" she asked, somehow managing to hide her smile as she glanced down at her body. Shrugging, she picked up the balloons, all of which either said *Good Luck,* or *Congratulations.* "It's the outfit you picked for me."

"The hell I did," he growled, coming out from behind the counter. "Take it off right now, or I swear to motherfuck—"

"Language!" their father said, again appearing out of nowhere.

How did he *do* that?

Caleb gestured toward Kassidy. "Have you *seen* her?"

Her father lowered his inventory sheet and frowned. "Why are you dressed like that and carrying balloons?"

"I lost a bet," she said drily. "I have to go sing to a customer."

"God help him," her dad muttered, crossing himself.

"Nice."

"Who cares about that? She's practically naked," Caleb hissed. "You win. I'll do it. Go get changed."

Kassidy grabbed the door handle, which she'd backed up to while he'd been freaking out. "I can't. A deal's a deal, right?"

With that, she pushed outside and took off for her car. Her smile didn't fade…until an old guy stepped into her path with cold eyes and a smirk as he looked her up and down, weighing her worth as if she were an object instead of a human.

He whistled at her through his teeth, giving her a once-over, and then a twice-over, and a thrice-over…if that was a thing. "Whatever you're selling, I'm buying."

"I'm not selling anything."

"Well, you should be," he said, leering at her.

Cheeks hot, she stepped around him and slid into her car, immediately locking the doors. After shoving all the balloons into the backseat, she glanced at the address on the paper. Some dude named Brett Ross was the person responsible for her debacle.

Him and Wyatt Hamilton's stupid arm.

Rolling her eyes, she punched the address into the

GPS and then frowned when she realized it was an affluent neighborhood just outside of town. Great. Just great. Not only did she get to make a fool out of herself, but she got to do it in front of some rich girl who would laugh about it later with her equally rich friends. Brett Ross probably ordered these balloons for his rich girlfriend who had amazing hair and even more amazing shoes.

"You wanted to live?" she said to herself. "Start driving."

Heart pounding, she put the windows down to enjoy the unseasonably warm fall day, turned up her favorite Broadway musical, and tried to keep up with the fast rhymes as she drove.

By the time she arrived at the mansion that held her doom, her hair was crazy, her palms sweaty, and she was two seconds from driving in the other direction and taking up her brother's offer to do it instead. But pride ran deep in the Thomas family, and she'd stupidly agreed to the bet, so she would pay the piper.

Groaning, she flipped the visor down and glanced at herself. Frowning, she tried to fix her hair, gave up, and pulled a tube of red lipstick out of her purse. Cleavage like this demanded sexy lips to match. After carefully applying the MAC shade, she glanced down at her feet. There was nothing she could do about the fact that she wore Chucks with her costume, but at least the rest of her fit the part.

She took her glasses off—if she had to make a fool of herself in front of some rich chick, at least it would be easier to do if she couldn't see the woman laughing at her. After wrestling the balloons out of the back, she smoothed the shirt of the costume over her stomach.

As she made her way up the stone walkway lined with carefully planted roses, she squinted up at a house that would easily fit three of her homes inside of it...maybe four. It had white shutters, a stone-faced front, and was gorgeous. In the garden, there was an Atlanta Saviors flag waving underneath the American flag that hung off the railing of the porch.

Glaring at it, she muttered, "This is all your fault."

After taking a deep breath, she lifted her hand and knocked on the door sharply, three times. It was time to make a complete and *utter* fool out of herself.

Chapter Two

Wyatt Hamilton frowned as he listened to the woman in his headphones tell him how to say hello. He'd tried his best, but no matter what he did, he screwed it up horribly. Groaning, he ripped out the earbuds and reclined on the couch cushions. All his life, he'd dreamed of a foreign endorsement, and his agent had never delivered. But the second he fired the asshole earlier today, fed up with the guy for never really caring about Wyatt's career more than he'd cared about his own, he'd been offered a deal by a company in China—and the dinner meeting was in a few hours.

There was no time to get a new agent.

No time to even *search*.

Since he didn't speak a single word in Chinese, he'd come up with the bright idea to try and learn, but that had been a complete failure. He was agentless, unable to communicate with the people interested in endorsing him, and was barely able to put on a damn tie by himself.

He was a complete and utter mess.

What the hell was he doing with his life?

"Son of a bitch," he muttered, picking up his phone when it buzzed.

His sister, Anna, had texted him. *So proud of you! Brett arranged a little surprise for you, by the way.*

Is it someone who can speak Chinese? he shot back immediately.

You wish. Relax, you'll be fine.

Wyatt sighed. *Funny, I feel like I'm going to make a fool out of myself. Does Brett speak Chinese?*

No.

Do you? He already knew the answer, but, hey, he was desperate.

NO.

Eric?

Eric is in Texas with his girlfriend. Maybe if you had a girlfriend, she would speak Chinese...

Wyatt rolled his eyes at the dig and set his phone down. His sister was constantly trying to set him up. She didn't seem to understand that he had no interest in a relationship, love, marriage, or children. All his life, there'd been only one goal—to play ball.

He'd traveled the country, kicked some ass, and dedicated his life to the game.

Football was his one true love. His life. His wife. His only long-term commitment. He had no interest in sharing his heart with anything or anyone else. The Saviors held the whole thing, and he liked it that way. He wasn't single by necessity. He was single by *choice*.

That was never going to change.

Just because his sister was engaged, one of his brothers was married, and his other brother was close to following in their footsteps, that didn't mean he had to follow suit. He and Cole were the last men standing.

That was just fine with him.

He'd leave the happily-ever-afters to his Hamilton siblings.

Someone knocked on the door three times, and he frowned. He wasn't expecting anyone and wasn't particularly in the mood to deal with someone showing up on his doorstep unannounced, either.

Placing his MacBook on the couch, he stood, stretched, and made his way to the door. He peeked through the peephole and stiffened. All he saw was a hell of a lot of balloons and a small, feminine hand holding them. "What the...?"

Slowly, he cracked the door open, half expecting this to be some sort of trap. When the woman didn't pounce on him and profess her undying love...he frowned. She didn't do anything. Just stood there, hiding behind balloons. When she didn't say anything, but just mumbled something under her breath, he cleared his throat. "Uh, can I help you, miss?"

"You're a *guy*?" She sighed. "Of *course* you're a guy."

"Is something wrong?"

"I just assumed since a guy sent a singing telegram that it was to a girl..."

He choked on a laugh. "Sorry?"

"Whatever, it's fine." Without moving the balloons, she said, "I'm here to deliver a singing telegram from Brett Ross. I'm so sorry."

Before he could ask her what she was sorry for, she opened her mouth and started singing...and he knew. *Fuck*, he knew. He'd heard dying cats that sounded more musically inclined than the woman hiding behind the balloons.

Swallowing hard, he stepped back into his house, fighting the urge to shut the door in her face. His mother had raised him to be polite, but Jesus, the girl could not *sing*. He gripped the knob, wincing, and forced his feet to stand still. As soon as she finished, he let out the breath he'd been holding, and said,

"Wow. Uh, thank you. Please, come in, place the balloons over there."

"Yes, sir," she mumbled, still hiding behind the balloons.

As he headed for his wallet so he could tip her, he said over his shoulder, "That was great, thanks."

"No, it wasn't. But thanks for lying." He heard her moving behind him, and then she said, "Again, I'm sorry. Here's the card that came with it and—" She broke off with a gasp when he turned around. "You're Wyatt *Hamilton*."

Even though he shouldn't have been surprised by her reaction to him—and he wasn't—he *was* surprised by his reaction to *her*. She wore a tiny green outfit that fit like it was painted on, her blond hair had been teased eighties-style, she had on dark red lipstick, and her body had more curves on it than an Alfa Romeo.

She was probably five-foot-two, but the way she held herself suggested she had a personality to match a much bigger frame. Her blue eyes were wide at first, but they quickly narrowed as she stepped backward. "It's...it's...*you*."

"It's me," he said slowly.

There was something about her, something intoxicating, that drew his eye and refused to let go. He wasn't sure what it was—it certainly wasn't her singing—but he simply had to find out. He especially wanted to know why she seemed to blame him for something, when they'd never met before. If they had, he would have remembered the way she twisted him up in knots without even trying.

"And you are...?" he said, drifting off and hoping she'd fill in the blank.

"Here because of you." She crossed her arms over her chest and tapped her foot. Her actions pushed her breasts up even more, and it took all his self-control not to gape at her like some pervert. The sight did make his jeans too tight around the zipper, though. "How's your arm, by the way?"

He frowned. "Uh…good."

"Obviously." She uncrossed her arms and stepped back again. "You can thank your rapidly healing arm for that little song you just endured. If you had just sat out *one* more game so your team could lose like a good sport, this never would have happened."

He cocked his head.

Lose? Sit out? Those words weren't in his vocabulary.

Most of the time when women met him and knew who he was, they asked for photos, or hyperventilated, or cried. This one *yelled* at him for his arm healing too fast, and for winning the game for his team. "What happened? Did you make a bet against me?"

"A terrible one," she muttered, pushing her hair out of her face distractedly. "Almost as bad as my singing."

"I thought your singing was lovely," he said, lying through his teeth and not regretting a single second. He crossed the room and stopped inches from her. She smelled like flowers and sunshine, if that even made sense. "It was definitely memorable, to say the least."

Slowly, he held out a twenty-dollar bill, locking eyes with her and refusing to let go.

"What's that for?" she asked.

"Your tip." His pulse sped up, and his fingers itched to touch her hair. Even as messy as it was, it looked softer than any flower petal he could ever touch. "It's a customary practice, and it's the least I can do for upsetting you by winning. I didn't peg you as a Pelicans fan."

"I'm not." She snorted and backed up again. "I love the Saviors."

He lifted a brow. "But you wanted us to lose?"

"No, of course not. But I thought you would be out, and without you—" She broke off, shaking her head slightly. "Anyway…yeah…thank you for choosing Thomas Florist."

She took one more step backward—which was a major mistake.

As she'd been busy telling him he sucked for winning, she hadn't noticed how close she was to the vase behind her.

He had two choices as she stumbled into it and lost her balance. He could catch her...or the priceless vase that had been in the Hamilton family since the eighteenth century.

Moving quickly, he caught her arm and hauled her against his chest, sucking in a breath as all her curves melded into his hard muscles, making him question everything he'd ever thought about instant attraction and chemistry. She rested her hands on his shoulders, gasping in through her perfectly red lips as the vase crashed to the floor behind her.

Fisting his shirt, she lifted her chin, staring at him.

"Oh no," she breathed.

He silently echoed her.

She was gorgeous. This close, the little dots of green in her blue eyes gave them an almost aqua appearance. Her hair touched his hand, and he confirmed that it was indeed as soft as he suspected. "Are you okay?"

"Yes, thank you." She lost her death grip on him. Glancing behind her, she groaned. "Oh my God, I'm so sorry. What did I break?"

"Nothing. It's fine," he said quickly.

"I took off my glasses so I couldn't see you laughing at me—"

"I'm not laughing at you," he said, frowning. "Why would I laugh at you?"

"And now I can't see a thing. The only reason I knew who you were was because *everyone* knows who you are, and you're gorgeous and even cuter in person, which isn't *fair*, but now I'm breaking shit, and singing horribly, and yelling at Wyatt Hamilton for winning and being amazing, and you're touching me, and you're amazing, and so frigging hot, and I need to *shut up.*"

His lips twitched. Her babbling was adorable, and quite frankly, she could carry on for as long as she wanted, as long as he got to hold her soft body against his while she did so. "I think you're doing just fine. Keep going. How hot am I?"

"Oh my—" she said again, rolling her eyes and flipping her hair over her shoulder. She still didn't move out of his arms. "Please tell me whatever just broke behind us isn't valuable."

He swallowed hard, lying through his teeth. "It wasn't valuable."

"*Whew.*" She craned her neck, glancing at it. "I can't see. What is it?"

"Just an empty vase."

She gasped again. She seemed to be big on that. Gasping. He'd rather make her gasp over something a hell of a lot naughtier than some broken glass on the floor. "No one puts an empty vase on a table by itself like that unless it's valuable. How much do I owe you?"

He blinked. "Uh...."

"Tell me." She stepped out of his arms, letting go of him instantly, and he did the same, even though he didn't really want to. Something about having her in his arms had seemed nice. "How much?"

"I don't want your money, ma'am." He stepped back, curling his fists at his sides, and forced a smile. "It's fine. An honest mistake. It could have happened to anyone."

"How much?" she repeated, touching her sides where her pockets would have been, but coming up empty. "I can run out to my car and—"

"It's fine. Like I said, I don't want your money." He dragged a hand through his hair and laughed. His phone lit up with a calendar reminder of his dinner with his possible investors, which immediately made his mood darken because he was going to have to go back to listening to that woman speak and failing to comprehend it. "But, hey, if you know someone who speaks Chinese, I'd gladly take them as repayment, though," he said jokingly.

Half jokingly.

Okay, fine, not jokingly at all.

She hesitated, tipping her head adorably to the side. "Take them...in what way? Are you going to lock them in your basement and keep them as collateral? Sell them on the black market?"

"Of course not," he said immediately, heat flushing through his veins as he laughed uneasily. "I'd just...borrow them. I have a dinner later on, and it's with Chinese men who are interested in possibly endorsing me, but I can't speak their language. I'm trying, but incapable of wrapping my head around it. I just wish I could have learned fast as a sign of friendship or whatever. Greet them in their own tongue."

She blinked at him.

He shifted his weight on his feet.

Had he sounded like an incapable idiot?

'Cause he was one.

When she remained silent, he forced a smile and said, "Honestly, though, it's not a big deal. It's just a vase."

"What time?" she asked slowly, her chest heaving erratically.

"Huh?"

"What time would you need me for this dinner?" she asked, her cheeks almost the same shade as her lips.

"You speak Chinese?" he asked, his heart picking up speed for more than one reason.

She nodded hesitantly.

"Fluently?"

If she was the answer to his prayers, not only would he be able to attend this dinner with someone who could carry on long conversations with his potential investors, but he'd get more time with this bewitching beauty that called to him like no other woman had before.

She nodded once, jerkily. "*Mao mao lin*."

"*Yes*." He caught her hand excitedly, his fingers rough against her much smoother skin, caught up in the excitement of the possibility of greeting his potential sponsors properly. The biggest thing in this game was respect, and what better way to say it than *mao mao lin*? "Are you sure you don't mind? Please don't feel like you have to. I was just kidding."

Mostly.

"Please. It's the least I could do," she said, waving a hand dismissively. "What time, and what attire?"

"Eight, and you could wear that if you want," he said, grinning because he'd lucked out when she knocked on his door today, in more ways than one. "It's…fetching."

She crossed her arms again and stared at him.

Dead ass stared.

He cleared his throat, losing the grin he'd been wearing since she spoke Chinese. "Uh…wear a dress, I guess?"

"Got it." She tucked her hair behind her ear nervously, glancing at him then lowering her gaze. "Like, ball gown, sundress, or cocktail dress?"

Shit. He had no clue what kind of dress was what. Ask him how best to throw a fifty-yard pass in an easterly ten mile-per-hour wind, and he'd be golden. "Like, one that goes like this…" he ran a line down his shoulders, showing a tank top, "and maybe stops like here?" he touched his thigh above his knee. "Pretty fabric, but not, like, diamonds, or anything like that."

Her lips curved into a smile. It was the first time she'd smiled since walking into his life, and it was breathtaking. There was no other word for it. "So…cocktail?"

"Sure, yeah. Cocktail." He ran a hand through his hair,

laughing uneasily because he couldn't understand what it was about her that kept throwing him off balance. He'd been around a lot of women, most of them beautiful, but this one… she was different. *Why*? "I'll be wearing a black suit and a tie."

"Got it."

Forcing his eyes off her, he crossed the room and picked up his phone. "Can I have your address? I'll pick you up on the way there."

She hugged herself. "I could just meet you there, if it's easier."

"I'll pick you up." He unlocked his phone, opened his contacts, and glanced at her. "Address?"

"S-Sure." She followed him into his living room. She glanced around a little bit, but considering she'd admitted to being basically blind without her glasses, he could only assume she wasn't actually seeing anything—just avoiding him because she was nervous, which was endearing. "Five-twenty Forty-Sixth Street, right in the middle of Atlanta."

"Great." He typed in the address quickly. "And your phone number?"

She spouted it off to him, her voice trembling.

"Thank you." His finger hovered over the place to put her name, and it occurred to him that she'd never actually given it to him. He glanced up, his heart hitching in his throat when he saw her biting down on her plump lower lip. It was innocent and yet sexy at the same time. "And…uh…your name, ma'am?"

She laughed uneasily. "Oh, yeah, I guess that would help. Kassidy. Kassidy Thomas."

"Great. I'm Wyatt Hamilton." He held his hand out to her. "Nice to meet you."

"I gathered," she said sarcastically. "I promise not to sing, by the way."

He laughed. "I told you, I enjoyed it."

"Sure." She gestured at her body. "Also, be warned, I don't usually dress like this."

"How disappointing. It works for you."

"It does something, all right." She let go of his hand. "I'll see you at…?"

"Seven-thirty."

She nodded. "Okay." She took a step toward the door, then paused, her shoulders stiff. "Seriously, though, how much was that vase?"

"I can't really say. It's been in my family for years."

Choking on a laugh, she said, "Please don't tell me that Alexander Hamilton once owned it, or something insane like that."

"Well…" he said, wincing.

"Shit, you're kidding, right?"

"It's fine," he said again. "It's just a vase."

She covered her face with her hands. "No, it's not. Like, what if Eliza gave that to him for his birthday, and it was his favorite, and he always put flowers from their garden in it to cheer her up after Phillip died because it was quiet uptown, and now I broke it because I'm stupid and took off my glasses—?"

Clearly, someone was a fan of *Hamilton*.

"Kassidy," he said softly, capturing her hands and pulling them down gently.

She froze with wide eyes. "Yeah?"

"I don't give a damn about the vase." Her skin under his was electrifying, and he stepped closer, instinctively craving more. There was this invisible pull between them, this undeniable lure, and all he wanted was to sweep her into his arms and see if she tasted as good as he was pretty sure she would. "I assure you, having you at my dinner with me is a hell of a lot more valuable to me than some stupid piece of glass that Alexander owned. Okay?"

She swallowed hard, her blue eyes still locked on his. Her lips were parted, and every breath that escaped tickled the skin of his throat. There was a heat to her eyes, a spark of attraction that told him she wasn't immune to that weird pull between them—if anything, maybe she was being pulled, too, which did nothing to help him cool the hell off. "O-okay."

"I'll see you at seven thirty?" he asked, his voice lowering for some reason.

She nodded. "Yeah. Sure."

"I look forward to our date…" he said, lowering his voice even more. "Kassidy."

She pulled free and ran, leaving behind nothing but balloons, a faint whiff of flowers and perfume…and a shattered, priceless Hamilton vase. Speaking of which…

His mother was going to *kill* him.

Chapter Three

This was not, and never would be, a real *date*.

No matter what Wyatt Hamilton had said earlier, this was just repayment for breaking his personal property, and nothing else. Guys like Wyatt didn't date shy, normal girls like her, and that's all there was to it. He'd called it a date out of habit, or perhaps to be kind, but they *both* knew she wasn't his type.

She kept reminding herself of that, because he was due to arrive at her house any minute now. After all, she'd seen the pictures of him with his endless parade of women on his arm. He never kept any around for long, but each one was always prettier than the last, as if he was trying to one-up himself in dating as well as on the field, and it was clearly working. He preferred tall, leggy, skinny, drop-dead gorgeous supermodels who owned the runway and the world around it.

Even if he did, for some reason, find her slightly attractive, she would never, ever, *ever* in a million years believe it, or act on it, or even really see it.

That didn't stop her from thinking about it, though.

Even for just a second.

And, boy, was she thinking about it…and him.

Biting down on her lip, she leaned closer to the mirror and opened her eyes wide as she applied her second coat of mascara. Date or not, she wanted to fit the part to repay her clumsy shattering of a historical vase. This particular brand of mascara claimed that it would increase lash-length tenfold with two coats, and long lashes never hurt a girl while groveling, right?

Her best friend, Jessica Franze, sighed from the bed and flopped back on it. "I can't believe you're going on a date with Wyatt Hamilton."

"It's not a date," Kassidy said, switching eyes. "It's a debt I owe him."

"Call it what you want, but in ten minutes, Wyatt Hamilton will be at your doorstep, ringing your bell, and taking you out to dinner at a fancy restaurant where they probably charge three figures for a plate." Jessica sat up again and pointed at her. "I don't know about you, but I call that living, my friend."

Jessica was the only other person privy to Kassidy's decision to stop being so careful about everything all the time, and she was right. No matter what this was called, she was going out with Wyatt Hamilton, bachelor quarterback for Atlanta, and that was a *huge frigging deal*.

Grinning, she lowered the wand. "Yeah, it is, isn't it?"

"Are his eyes as blue as they seem on TV?"

She sighed, picturing them. She couldn't help it. "Even bluer."

"Not possible."

"Oh, but it is." She grinned. "And they sparkle when he laughs. Like, actually sparkle. His hair is blonder, too. Not light blond, but not quite brown. You know?"

Jess nodded. "Mm-hm."

"And his muscles…" She sighed again. "*Ugh.*"

So frigging big.

"I'm so jealous," Jessica said, her eyes wide. "What if you're on blogs and on the news?"

Jessica had been single for a year now, after her boyfriend had cheated on her and left her. She'd been firmly on the men-suck bandwagon with Kassidy ever since.

Butterflies flew in her stomach. The idea of the world seeing her at Wyatt's side was an unsettling one, at best. What must it be like to be in the spotlight like that? To always have to wonder if you'd end up on TMZ? It must be crazy. No wonder he only dated supermodels, who were used to the pressure.

Women like Samantha Ford, who had been named the hottest Playboy model of the year, and had been on his arm for last week's *Quarterbacks Give Back* gala in New York City. The media speculated that this was the real thing and that Wyatt Hamilton had fallen, and fallen hard, for the lingerie model.

"I hope not."

"But that would be fun," Jessica argued. "Something to show your future grandkids. 'This is when Nana was young and pretty and dated a star quarterback.'"

"Embellishment, much?" Kassidy asked.

Did he and Samantha keep in touch?

Would he be texting her during their "date"?

Why do you care? She didn't. Not really.

Jessica shrugged. "History is told by the victor. And honey? You're winning."

"If you say so…" Kassidy capped her mascara and studied herself in the mirror, squinting. Letting out a sigh, she picked up her glasses and slid them into place so she could see again.

Yeah, she wouldn't be going sans glasses again.

She couldn't afford to break something else.

She'd opted for a tight-fitting red dress, a pair of black heels, and had curled her hair and left it down again. Uncharacteristically, she'd applied heavy gray eye makeup and pink lipstick. If nothing else, she looked the part of the arm candy she would be, and that was all she could ask for. She'd do her best to try and make up for the property she destroyed, and that was all she could offer him. Hopefully, it would be enough.

But *still*.

Stupidly, she couldn't shake the anticipation that built in her stomach and made her fingers tingle and her breath come quickly. There was no denying that she was nervous and excited to go out with Wyatt, and she just had to accept that a small, girlish part of her mind would view this as a date, no matter what the bigger, more logical part of her brain said.

"I'll go, so I don't cramp your style." Jessica stood and swooped up the other dresses she'd brought along, since Kassidy hadn't owned anything fancy or sexy enough for dinner with Wyatt Hamilton. "Good choice on the dress, by the way."

"Thank you for letting me borrow it," Kassidy said, smoothing the fabric over her stomach. It was a lower neckline than she usually wore, but not quite as bad as the Peter Pan costume. It showed a hint of cleavage, was sleeveless, made of the softest cotton she'd ever found, and hit right above the knee, pretty much replicating what Wyatt had requested earlier today, which was why she picked it.

Hopefully he liked it…not because she cared what he thought or anything, but because she owed him a shit ton of money. Or so she kept telling herself.

Jessica hugged her with her free arm. "You're going to do great. Text me after and tell me if he's an asshole…and if he smells good. I bet he smells good."

"He does." She'd learned that earlier when he saved her

from hitting the floor. Being in his arms, against his hard chest, had been life-changing.

How could muscles *be* so hard?

"Like, really good."

Jessica let out a sigh. "No fair."

"You can stay and meet him if you want," she said, letting go of her friend. "I'm sure he wouldn't mind."

"No."

"But—" she started.

"*No.*" Jess started for the door. "Did you tell Caleb that you're going out with him?"

Like usual, Jess blushed a little when she mentioned Kassidy's older brother. She was 99 percent certain her best friend had a thing for Caleb, even though she'd never admit it. "Nope. I didn't even tell him that Wyatt was the one I delivered balloons to. If he knew, he'd be here, waiting to meet him first and warn him that his sister is off-limits second. Then he'd be showing up at his house, since he has the address, and he'd never leave the poor guy alone."

"Maybe." Jessica grinned. "Maybe his favorite football player is the one person he'd leave alone when it comes to his sister."

"Right," Kassidy muttered, smoothing her hair one last time. "I'm nervous."

"Don't be. He'll love you. How could he not?"

"I don't want him to love me, I just don't want to make a fool out of myself in front of him." She winced, remembering that awful song she'd delivered. "Again."

"You won't." Jessica walked out the bedroom door. "Call me as soon as you're alone."

"Love you," Kassidy called out.

"Love you more," Jess said over her shoulder.

The front door opened and shut. She let out a breath, checking herself out in the mirror, critically taking in every detail. Her dress was too tight. She was breathing too rapidly. The world closed in around her, suffocating her, threatening to choke her, but she had nothing to be worried about...

Because she was *not* going on a date with Wyatt Hamilton.

• • •

He'd never been this nervous before. As he pulled up to a charming house, his palms were sweatier than they were the time he'd brought his team to victory in the Super Bowl, and his heart raced like he'd sprinted down the field full-speed, with the other team's fastest player hot on his heels. It was ridiculous.

He didn't even *know* this woman.

Why did she make him all shaky and weird inside?

All he really knew about her was that she sang horribly, wore a Peter Pan/Tinkerbell costume like no one else, and had broken a vase that had been in his family for more generations than hours he'd known her. And yet it was still like he was a schoolkid on his first date.

"Pull yourself together, Hamilton," he muttered under his breath.

He flexed his hands on the wheel. Her house was cute. It had white siding, shuttered windows, and a small porch out front. She'd left the light on for him. He wasn't sure why, but it warmed his heart that she'd thought of him like that. Swallowing hard, he tugged at his tie, cursed under his breath, and opened his car door.

After grabbing the flowers, he made his way up to her door. Before he could even knock, it swung open, and for the second time that day, she took his breath away.

How did she keep doing that?

She'd been sexy in her costume, but in her red dress, she was downright dangerous to his focus, something he generally avoided like the plague. Anything that took his focus off his game and his stats was dangerous. Yet here he was.

At her door.

Only because I need her for the meeting. After he wooed his potential investors, with her help, he'd politely thank her for her assistance, drop her off at her door, and never see her again.

"Hey," she said breathlessly.

"Hi. You look…" He checked her out again. *Bad idea.* Every inch of red fabric clung to her generous curves, and he ached to trace each and every one. Most of the women he dated were tall, curve-free, and barely ate half a salad at dinner. They deferred to him like he was some sort of god— but being on her doorstep made him wonder idly if he'd been dating the wrong kind of women all these years. "Wow."

"Thanks," she said, nervously tucking her hair behind her ear and stepping back so he could go inside. "Come in. I just need to grab my purse and jacket, and then I'll be ready to go."

He swallowed past his dry throat and walked past her. She smelled like flowers again. The scent of her perfume was equal parts torturous and delicious. Her scent put the flowers he brought her to shame. Speaking of which… "Here you go."

"You got me…flowers?"

"From your shop, yes," he said, forcing a smile. "I told the guy behind the counter that you did a fine job singing, too, so don't worry about that."

She closed her eyes. "Did you tell him they were for me?"

"No." He frowned. "Why?"

"Did he fanboy all over you?" she asked, ignoring his question.

"Yeah…" He laughed and eyed her from under his lowered head as he ducked down shyly. Fangirling always left him a little uncomfortable. He appreciated it, and loved his fans, but he never knew what to say, or how to act, when someone was gushing all over him. "He was nice. I think his name was…Caleb?"

"Yep. Caleb." She took the flowers, her fingers brushing his. "My brother. Sorry about that."

"*Oh*." He scratched his head, smiling. "So, the guy he called Dad…?"

"My dad." She laughed. "You basically just met my family, minus my mother."

"Before the first date?" He rubbed the back of his neck and glanced around. "A little unorthodox, but okay."

Her place was sparsely furnished, but every piece seemed to him to have been picked out with a lot of thought. He was pretty sure a girl like Kassidy never did anything without considering all her options.

For some reason, he wanted to challenge that self-control.

"It's not a date," she said quickly, her cheeks flushing. "It's a debt owed."

He didn't say anything.

It was, absolutely, a motherfucking *date*.

"I probably don't need to tell you this, since you're a pro and all, but you should put those in water before we go," he said, gesturing at the red roses.

He'd decided to go classic.

She seemed like a classic kind of girl.

"Uh…right." She headed for the kitchen, and he watched her go, placing his hands in his pockets. "You're sure you didn't mention me, or that we were going on a…thing…to my brother, right?"

"I think I'd remember," he said, laughing at her careful avoidance of the word *date*. "I just said you came by, sang for me, and did great. At the time, I thought I was putting a good word in for you with your employer. If I'd known he was your brother, I never would have even mentioned it."

"I wish you hadn't, because—" She broke off and muttered under her breath. Her phone went off on the counter, next to her purse, and she frowned down at it. "And there's the text."

"What text?" he asked, confused.

"The one I knew I'd be getting from my brother."

"Oh. What does it say?" he asked slowly, walking toward her.

Her kitchen had white cabinets, a gray, tiled backsplash, and granite countertops. He liked it. It was very clean. Very organized. Very *her*.

"Do you ever do anything spur of the moment?" he asked.

She blinked at him, clearly caught off guard by his question.

"Uh…not really, no."

"I figured." He smiled at her. "The text?"

"Huh?" she asked, still taken aback by him.

Good. At least he wasn't alone.

"The text." He gestured at her phone. "What does it say?"

She read it. "That I should have told him I broke the ears of the greatest quarterback to ever live," she said. "Followed by demands for every detail about you."

He snorted. "Every?"

"*Every*," she returned, lowering her phone. "He's kind of a big fan."

"I hadn't noticed."

She laughed. Turning toward him with a smile, she said, "Yeah, sure you didn't. Just like I was a good singer, and I'm not in debt to you after breaking your vase. You, Wyatt Hamilton, are a liar. A nice one, but a liar nonetheless."

He was unable to speak or defend himself, because when she smiled, she lit up the room. It was his goal, then and there, to make her smile as much as he could, all night long, before he walked away from her. "I don't lie. I always tell the truth. So, it's true when I say this: you're beautiful. When you smile, I swear, you take my breath away."

She froze with the vase she'd pulled out from the cabinet halfway to the countertop. Slowly, she set it down and turned his way again, trembling. "You don't have to do that."

Closing the distance between them, he took the flowers out of her hand and took the wrapping off, since she didn't seem to be doing it herself. "Do what?"

"Pretend to be interested in me like that," she said, snatching the flowers back, shoving them gently in the vase and then filling it with water. "I'm going out with you because I happen to speak the right language. This isn't a date, and these flowers don't mean anything, and I'm not your type, and you're not attracted to me in the slightest, so we can just go to this dinner as—"

"I mean no disrespect, Kassidy, but..." He stepped directly behind her, slowly spun her around, and locked eyes with her. "Where do you get off telling me whether or not I find you attractive? I think I would know better than you."

"Yeah, sure, but..." She fidgeted with her hands in front of her stomach. It was charmingly endearing, her nervousness around him. All the other women he spent time with tried to play it cool, to act like they didn't care who he was or what he did, but she didn't hide her feelings at all. He sensed what was going on in her mind, and she was so very real. "How's Samantha?"

"Who?" he asked, frowning.

He hadn't seen that question coming on the next page.

"Samantha Ford."

He laughed. "Good, I guess. I mean, I haven't spoken to her since last week, but I'd hope her week is going well."

"So, you're not...?"

"An item?" He shrugged, not surprised she'd believed

the fodder the press liked to spread about him. They were almost as desperate to pair him off with a woman as his sister Anna was. "Nah. I'm not looking for that."

"For what?" she asked, crinkling her nose up adorably.

"That." He lifted a hand, touching her shoulder and skimming his fingers down her smooth skin. He hadn't meant to, but really, he couldn't help it. She was so soft and beautiful, with bright eyes and soft lips. "Love. Girlfriends. Relationships."

She gasped, her cheeks reddening and her body swaying toward him in an open invitation for more. "*O-Oh.*"

He moved his fingers back up her arm, watching the goose bumps rise on her skin. They were almost as mesmerizing as she was. If he pressed against her and whispered in her ear, would more come up all over her?

"Wyatt."

"Yes?" he asked, snapping himself to attention and pulling his hand back.

Jesus, had he been touching her?

"I…we…if we're being honest about what we want, and who we are, then I have to tell you, touching me like that isn't going to get you anywhere."

His heart dropped. If he'd made her uncomfortable, he'd never forgive himself. He had no clue what had gotten into him, besides the fact that she was drop-dead gorgeous, and he wanted her more than he ever wanted anyone. "I'm so sorry. I never meant to… If you're not comfortable going out with me, I completely understand."

"No, no. It's not like that. It was…nice."

He hesitated. "It was?"

"Yes, of course, but I'm not that kind of girl," she said, stepping back to put a safer distance between them.

He frowned. "What kind of girl?"

"The kind who kisses a guy she just met, who happens to

be famous, and I sure as hell am not spontaneous enough to kiss you without thinking about what comes next."

"What kind of girl are you, then? Tell me."

He had to know everything about her. Why? He had no idea.

"I'm overly cautious, never take risks, haven't been on a date in almost five years, and basically am pretty much the most boring person you'll ever meet. *Ever.*"

"You don't bore me," he said softly, unable to believe that this enchanting woman had, one, not been on a date in five years, and two, thought she was boring. Whoever she had dated last had seriously messed up if he'd left her feeling that way. "As a matter of fact, you intrigue me."

She laughed nervously. "Give it time. It'll wear off, and you'll see the truth." After grabbing her purse and her phone, she faced him again, hugging her items close to her chest, avoiding his eyes the whole time. "You ready to go get an endorsement deal?"

He was ready for a hell of a lot of things. Showing Kassidy Thomas she was the furthest thing from boring he'd ever seen was at the top of his list.

"I'm definitely ready."

He'd make sure she never doubted her worth, and she'd never forget the things he showed her—even though he'd never see her again.

Chapter Four

Oh. My. God. Wyatt Hamilton is touching me.

Between his fluttering touches on the side of her thigh, on her upper back, her hand, and the way he'd caressed her arm in her kitchen…she was starting to really, *really* want this to be a date, which was dangerous to her well-being. Guys like Wyatt probably ate girls like her for appetizers before moving on to the main course. Would he have tried to kiss her in her kitchen earlier if she hadn't stopped him? If so, would she have *let* him? The answer to that, before she had decided to live her life fully, would have been a resounding no.

But now…

She wasn't so sure.

Her money was on Wyatt being a hell of a kisser.

"More wine?" he asked, leaning close and picking up the bottle of Cabernet in the middle of the table.

"Yes, please," she said breathlessly.

He leaned even closer, filling her glass and resting a hand between her shoulder blades as he did so. His fingers burned through the thin fabric of her dress, marking her skin in ways she'd never forget. All these touches were PG rated and completely innocent, but they made her heart race as if he were pinning her to the wall and stripping her bare instead. It was as if he'd unlocked this ferocious beast inside of her that demanded he do things to her that she'd only ever dreamed about.

"There you go," he murmured, shooting her a sexy smile.

She took a deep breath. "Thank you."

He nodded once, then turned his focus to the men across the table from them. They'd been discussing business for most of the meal now, and they were all waiting for dessert to be delivered. She'd interjected a few times, but they spoke English well, and there wasn't much need for a translator, so she'd kept her linguistic skills mostly to herself, other than her greeting to them at the beginning of the meal.

"And how, exactly, would that be portrayed in your country?" Wyatt asked. His blond hair was swept to the side tonight and held in place with some sort of product. His hard jaw seemed even more defined when he was dressed in a suit—which made no sense, but whatever—and when he smiled, dimples popped out. Actual frigging *dimples*.

She'd been too blind to see those before.

The businessmen leaned forward, clearly also sensing the shift in the mood that said it was time to get to business. "We would advertise on the best shows, in the evening, and everyone would see you. We are big fans of American football, and we all follow the biggest quarterbacks." He smiled and gestured at Wyatt. "And the ladies love the handsome ones, yes?"

Wyatt's cheeks flushed slightly. "Well…"

"Yes," she interjected, placing a hand on his arm. It was even harder than she remembered. She'd never *met* a man with muscles like this up close and personal. "We do love the handsome ones."

He turned and locked eyes with her, and the breath she'd been inhaling stuck in her throat. His eyes dipped down her body slowly, thoroughly, as if...as if...he had every intention of doing what she'd only fleetingly fantasized about earlier, pressing her against a wall and stripping her bare.

And, God help her, she *wanted* him to.

"Did you just call me handsome, Kass?" he asked quietly.

"Duh," she said under her breath for him, before smiling at the men across from her and raising her voice. "And handsome sells, does it not?"

"It does," the older man said, nodding at her. "As does beauty such as yours."

Her cheeks heated. "Thank you."

"We have prepared an offer we think you will find very generous. If you'll give us a moment to confer?"

Wyatt gestured toward them. "Of course."

The older man spoke to his partner, expressing concern that she might understand them. She kept her face blank and tried to pretend like she didn't. They said something shocking about her breasts, watching closely to see if she reacted.

She didn't so much as flinch.

If they were testing out her linguistic skills, she wanted to hear every word, thank you very much. Satisfied, they nodded and said she clearly didn't understand them. She held her breath as they talked about lowering their offer since he didn't have an agent to speak for him at the moment. She stiffened as they dropped the number significantly, and then they laughed because their investors would more than likely give them a bonus for their smart strategy.

She listened in, weighing the pros and cons of speaking up and telling them she was fully aware that they were about to try and con a good man out of money. She had come along to translate, if necessary, but did this fall under that category? If Wyatt knew what they were saying, would he want her to intervene on his behalf? If she did, would it go well? Or would she be better off keeping her mouth shut and keeping her nose out of his business?

It wasn't her place to negotiate for him.

He hadn't asked her to do that.

The older man smiled at Wyatt. "We are prepared to offer you—"

Shit. She couldn't do it. Couldn't let them rip off a good man like Wyatt. "I don't think you want to make that offer just yet," she interrupted in Chinese.

Wyatt stiffened. "What did you just say to them?"

"Shh." She said, placing her hand on his thigh and squeezing. She tried her best not to get distracted by how hard it was, but *hot damn*. She switched back to Chinese. "I think we need to renegotiate, gentlemen. He might not have an agent right now, but he has me."

The older man blanched, his eyes wide. "You understood us?"

"Yes, I understood everything." She held his gaze. "*Everything.*"

"Ma'am, I'm sorry—" he started.

"I'm sure, but that isn't what I want to talk about." She nodded once toward Wyatt. "He is worth more than what you're offering. He's unaware that you tried to shortchange him, and he doesn't need to find out, if you make this right."

The younger man laughed and tugged on his tie. "Why should we offer him full price, when he is unrepresented, and this is a huge deal for him—as he's already stated?"

"Because it's a huge deal for you, too." She crossed her arms. "This would bring in a lot of revenue for you, as no one else had secured an athlete of his caliber in your field yet. Wyatt Hamilton is a household name, and I have every reason to believe by the time this season is over, everyone who hasn't heard of him yet *will*."

Wyatt sat up straighter, clearly tired of not understanding a single word that was being spoken around and about him. "Kass—"

"Quiet." She squeezed his leg again and switched to Chinese, "He's getting restless. Tell me what I want to hear, gentlemen. Make it better than your original offer, since you were so quick to turn on him when you thought he was weak."

The younger guy's jaw dropped. "You can't be serious."

"Dead. Go on, then. He's waiting."

After issuing her threat, she picked up her wine and took a big gulp because she might have just stepped out-of-bounds. He'd brought her here to help him translate if necessary, not to negotiate his offer. If these men walked away from him right now, it would be her fault, and she'd owe him for a busted endorsement deal, on top of a priceless vase.

What had she *done*?

The older man laughed, leaning back in his chair. He switched back to English effortlessly, looping Wyatt back into the conversation. "You have quite the ferocious defender as your companion, Mr. Hamilton. She's like a dog with a bone, only ten times as fierce."

Wyatt cleared his throat, side-eying her. "Yes, she is… something else."

She shifted in her seat, refusing to back down. She'd made her play, for better or for worse, against her better judgment, and she was going to stick to it. "I'm just looking out for the best interests of everyone here at this table."

"Indeed," the gentleman said. "After your companion's… wise…words, we are prepared to offer you"—he scribbled down a number on a business card and slid it toward them— "this much, which is almost double our original offer. We appreciate a hard-baller almost as much as we appreciate a good deal, and this falls into both categories."

Wyatt held it out to her, showing her. She glanced at it

and nodded the verification he seemed to desire that it was, indeed, almost double the number the men had been prepared to offer—and *holy crap, that was a lot of money.* More than she'd ever seen, or would see, in her life. He smiled and tucked the card into the breast pocket of his jacket. "Gentlemen, I do believe we have a deal."

They stood and shook hands.

Everyone clapped one another on the back in that way that men always did, and she swallowed another gulp of wine because *she did it.* She took a chance, spoke up, and it worked. One might say that by choosing to interject herself into the situation, she'd been living life to its fullest. Living wasn't so hard after all, was it?

Guess she didn't owe him for that vase anymore.

With this *win*, came a heady rush of victory unlike any other she had ever experienced. *Never again.* Never again would she put herself behind a wall or inside a bubble because some jerk had made her doubt herself. Never again would she stop living, or forget to take risks like she'd taken. Never again would she forget that for one night and one night only, she'd gone on a date with Wyatt Hamilton, or that she'd scored him a deal that would leave him sitting on a big wad of cash for the rest of his long, healthy life—all with her quick wits and sharp brain.

This was living.

She could *fly* over the white puffy clouds, higher than the planes in the blue sky.

And she was never going touch the ground again.

Smiling, she took another drink. Tomorrow, she was going to go to that spinning class at her gym that she always wanted to try but had been too nervous to actually go. She'd been sure she would make a fool out of herself, since everyone else always just seemed to know what to do and she didn't, but screw that. She was going.

After that, she'd go get those highlights she'd been eyeing for a few months but had been too scared to try. Maybe she'd even join that dating site Jess kept telling her they should try out together for fun. The time was now. She'd waited long enough.

Wyatt placed a hand on her back. "Kass?"

She jerked back to the present, and back to admiring the sexiest eyes she'd ever seen on a man. He had a way of looking at a girl that made her forget all logic, and left her trembling and aching for something only he could give her. Did he see the effect he had on women, or was he blind to the full extent of his sexual allure?

Oh, who was she kidding? He knew.

"Yeah?" she asked.

"That was amazing," he said, running his hand up and down her spine in an intoxicatingly seductive way, but she wasn't even sure he realized he was doing it. Everywhere he touched tingled and burned and ached for more. "You started talking, and I wasn't sure what was happening, but holy shit, you pulled it off."

"You're not mad at me for interjecting myself into the situation?" she asked slowly.

"Mad?" He laughed. "Hell no. You got me a great deal, with loads of money and opportunity. What the hell do I have to be angry about?"

"In that case…" She tucked her hair behind her ear and smiled. "Glad to help."

"Smart and sexy as hell," he said, still grinning and shaking his head. "You're the whole package."

She bit her tongue. "You don't have to do that."

"Do what?" he said, his voice sharp.

"Say those things. I was just paying back a debt owed."

"Here we go again," he said, his tone a little hard. "I fail to see why you find it so hard to believe I am attracted to you.

Your hair is the softest I've ever seen, and I've been dying to touch it all night." He slid a few strands through his fingers. "Behind those red-rimmed glasses of yours, your eyes are a gorgeous shade of blue that pulls me in. As if that's not enough, your mind is brilliant, and around you, I can just be a normal guy, with a normal girl, out on a normal date, and that's pretty amazing, too. I can't remember the last time that happened."

She shivered, swaying toward him slightly. "That's because you're not normal. You're Wyatt Hamilton."

"And you're Kassidy Thomas."

Exactly. She was just Kassidy Thomas, while he was... well, everyone knew what he was. She didn't speak, because what was she supposed to say to that?

"Again, thank you for helping me out. Are you ready for me to take you home now?" He hesitated, then added, "Or, if you'd like, maybe we could pick up a bottle of champagne on the way and celebrate at your place before I go?"

Wyatt Hamilton, arguably the hottest guy in all the NFL, was asking her to have a drink with him, in her home, and she had no doubt what that drink could lead to if she accepted... she was ready for that. Whatever the hell happened from all of this, she was so there.

Against all logic and reason, *she was there.*

She wanted to live? Well, here was her chance.

Trembling, she picked up her glass, downed the rest of her wine, and for once in her life refused to think something through, because if she thought it through, there was no way she would say: "Sounds great. I know the perfect place to stop along the way."

Chapter Five

They walked up to her door, his hand at her lower back, guiding her. The whole ride home, she'd been silent at times, biting her lower lip, not meeting his eyes. At other times, she would talk endlessly about anything—the traffic, the people waiting to cross, hell, even the weather. There was no hiding the fact she was nervous, and he'd attempted to set her mind at ease with a little bit of light humor, but every time he tried, she went right back to fidgeting.

What the hell did she think he was going to do to her?

They were just sharing a bottle of champagne.

Thing was, though, she wanted more—and so did he. He'd seen that flare of excitement in her eyes when he told her he found her undeniably sexy, and there was no doubt in his mind that she wanted him as badly as he wanted her. She was just too nervous to *act* on it.

For some reason, tonight, he was, too.

She made him nervous. *Him*. Wyatt Hamilton.

As she slid her key into the lock, her hands trembled, and he bit back a smile, stepping behind her, making sure to keep his body a safe distance from hers. "You smell like flowers."

"Yeah, I'm always around them. Sometimes it seems like no matter how hard I try, I can't get rid of the scent, so I stopped trying and decided to roll with it."

"It works for you." He touched her hair gently.

She let out a ragged breath. "Your cologne works for you, too. And your clothes. Your hair. Your face…"

"My face?" he asked, laughing.

"Yep. Your face." She skimmed her fingernails up his arm, under his suit jacket. It made his cock harden and swell, and he stepped slightly closer, aching to press against her from behind, yet holding himself back. "And these. Your muscles. They're working for you, too."

He chuckled. "Thank you."

"You're welcome." With a smile, she fell silent, not opening her door, not pulling away, but not moving closer to him, either.

"Are you going to let me in?"

"Huh?" she asked breathlessly. "*Oh*. Yeah."

She opened the door and gestured him inside.

He was a gentleman, so he motioned for her to go first.

Frowning, she motioned for him to go again.

He did the same.

She laughed nervously, rolling her eyes, and dropped her hand. "Fine. You win, I'll go."

Grinning, he followed after her, shutting the door behind him with a soft *click*. "When it comes to duels of stubbornness, I'll always win. Just ask my brothers."

"You have brothers?" she asked quietly.

"Yep, three of them, and a sister, too." As she turned on the lights in her living room, he shifted the bottle of cold champagne to his left hand.

"Are you the baby?"

"Nah." He smiled. "That's my sister, Anna. I'm kind of

in the middle."

"The forgotten child," she joked, tipping her head toward the kitchen in silent invitation.

He snorted, following her. "Not in my family. No one was forgotten, despite the fact that there were five of us."

When she walked, her hips swayed, and he'd swear she was gracefully floating through the air. Her long blond hair fell down her back in waves, and he knew it felt better in his hands than a brand-new football. She made everything look so easy. So perfect.

"How about you?" he asked, his throat thick and almost choking him.

"Huh?" She pulled out glasses. "Oh. I'm the youngest."

"Any other siblings?" he asked politely.

"Nope, just the one."

He nodded, taking the champagne out of the bag and removing the gold foil before working on the cork. She'd picked it after he'd told her to choose whatever she wanted because he was paying for it, and it had been ridiculously cheap. Any other woman he took out would have picked only a top shelf item, but she'd kept it under fifteen dollars.

It had been refreshingly charming and a welcomed change of pace.

Maybe that was why he was here, having the type of personal conversation that he usually avoided, and trying to think of anything to say to make her laugh because she had one hell of a laugh and he needed to hear it as often as possible.

When the top popped, she jumped slightly, holding a hand to her chest and then laughing nervously. "That always gets me," she said, seemingly half in apology and half in amusement at herself.

Her cheeks were flushed and her lips parted, and she was breathtaking.

"Me, too," he said, not really thinking about the champagne.

"No, it didn't. You didn't even jump."

No, he hadn't. But she was making him just as jumpy as her, he was just better at hiding it. It was kind of his job to hide his nerves from his fans and his teammates, who looked to him as a leader.

Without saying anything, he poured them both a glass of bubbling champagne, then handed her the fuller one. Her fingers brushed his, and it took all his control not to let his touch linger even longer. He hadn't come here to seduce and forget her. He'd come to get to know her. To thank her.

Then he'd leave...without touching her.

Lifting his glass, he said, "To our successes."

"To our successes." She clinked her glass against his then lifted it to her pink, lush mouth. He could see the tip of her tongue as she drank. He'd never been so jealous of an inanimate object as he was of her glass right now. After lowering the drink, she licked her lips and asked, "Were you closer to one of your siblings than the others?"

He took a sip, thinking that over. "As kids, Anna or Chris were closest to me, I guess. But now, I'd say I'm closer to the others, and they're all about equal. I even helped Eric get his girl back a few months ago."

"How?" she asked, walking into the living room.

He followed her, grabbing the champagne for easy refilling purposes. "Long story short, they were sleeping together and swore not to let it get serious because she was moving. Well, it got serious, and instead of telling her he loved her, he let her leave for Texas because it was 'the right thing to do.'"

"Wow." She sat and leaned on her knees, pushing her breasts up. Any other girl, he'd think she did it to entice him, but with her, he doubted it. She seemed completely unaware of her charms, and how easy it would be for her to seduce him if she wanted. "What did you tell him to do?"

After setting the bottle of champagne down on a newspaper, he sat beside her, keeping a respectable distance between them to remind himself that he wasn't there to get her naked...even though he wanted to. "I told him to stop letting the love of his life leave, and to go win her back. So, he got out of his contract and moved to Texas for her."

She blinked, her mouth parted. "He did?"

"Yep, left his dream job and everything."

"He must really love her," she said slowly.

"I guess so," he said.

She eyed him. "You're not big on love?"

How had she figured that out? Was it in his tone? "Love is good."

"But you don't want it."

He shrugged. "I have it. My parents. My siblings. My team. My fans." He took a sip, then added, "To seek out more is just greedy, and to be honest, I don't want more."

She nodded, pursing her lips. "Why not?"

If anyone else asked, he'd give a generic answer, like: *too many beautiful people out there to commit to one for the rest of my life.* But with her, he wanted to be honest. "I love football. Love the game. The travel. The challenge. The wins. Even the losses. I love everything about it."

She played with a piece of her hair. "And...?"

"And if I fell in love with someone else, something I don't even think I'm capable of, then that would take away from the love I have for the game. It would pull me out of it. I'd start to resent the travel, the time away from home, and I'd lose my love for football." He set his glass down, trying to find the right words to express what he was trying to say. "I've seen it happen, time and time again. A player is on a path to MVP, and everyone is buzzing about him, but then he meets a girl, gets married, has kids…and all he wants is to rush home to his family every night. He stops training hard. Stops doubling up on gym time. And slowly but surely, he fades away."

She set her glass down, too, turning so her leg was folded under her. It made her dress ride up her thigh, something he tried really hard not to notice. He failed. Horribly. "That's not fair, though. Plenty of good players are married and still on the top of their game."

"Sure they are." He shrugged. "But lots aren't, too, and to be honest, that's not a risk I'm willing to take."

She nodded. "I understand."

"You do?"

"Of course." She bit her lip. "So, after you retire…would you be open to the idea of love then?"

"I can't say I really think about it. I've never been one to want someone with me, and I don't feel like I'm missing out on something because I don't have a partner at my side." He twisted his lips. "I've never wanted those things. Family. Love. Marriage. I don't think I ever will."

"I…I see." She reached out for her glass, but he hurried to beat her to it and hand it off. "Thank you."

"You're welcome," he murmured. "How about you? You want that special someone?"

Licking her lips, she glanced away, her cheeks flushed. "I guess, yeah. I haven't exactly been out there, dating or anything. It's been five years since I had a partner, as you called it."

He drank, taking a moment to reflect on that. "May I ask a personal question?"

"Sure."

"Why so long?" he asked slowly. "What happened?"

"Uh…well, to be honest, it was because of a guy."

"It's always because of a guy," he said drily.

"Yeah, I guess." She focused on the fireplace, even

though it wasn't lit. He watched her. Her lashes were long and dark. "We started dating in high school. We chose the same college. Made plans. We were going to graduate and move in together, then get engaged after a year. Married a year after that. Kids two years later. Three—two boys and a girl."

Damn, he'd never sat and planned out his life like that. All he knew was that he wanted to play ball, and he wanted to do it alone. Hell, most of the time he had no clue what he was going to do when he woke up on his days off, let alone for his whole life. "That's very...precise."

"I'm not a very impulsive person," she said, stating the obvious.

"I am. I don't really plan out things besides plays."

"I plan *everything*. Overthink everything. Go through every single scenario and the hundreds of ways it could end before making a choice. I don't jump into anything. I walk slowly, carefully, and am always ready to back out if needed."

He nodded, studying her, letting her gather her thoughts.

She smiled sadly. "Ever since he left, I stopped living. I haven't done anything risky or even slightly adventurous in a very long time."

The way she said it made him think she was trying to change that. "Why not?"

"Because of him, I guess. And me. And...life."

He shook his head. "What did he do to you?"

"Nothing, really. Like I said, I overthink everything. One day, he just had enough of me thinking all the time." She bit her lower lip. "He said I was boring him to death, and that if I ever decided to stop overthinking every single thing, to come find him. If I ever decided to step outside of my comfort zone, and maybe decide to be fun for once in my life, then he'd consider taking me back. Until then...he'd be with Becky."

He winced. "Who's Becky?"

"Some girl with big boobs and even bigger hair." She

smiled, but the smile didn't reach her eyes. "Someone who wasn't afraid to live. So, I decided, then and there, if I was so boring that I could make the man who'd sworn to love me for the rest of my life turn away from me…I just wouldn't date at all. I'd stay on my own. Take care of myself. And do things my way."

He shook his head. "The man was clearly a fool. You're not—"

"Yes, I am. Or, I was."

"And now?" he asked hesitantly.

"Now I want to live. Right before I met you, I promised that I'd stop hiding behind my past and the asshole who hurt me. I'm ready to move on. To try new things. To get back out there."

His chest tightened. "As in, dating."

"Yep. That, and other things."

The idea of her going out with some faceless dude didn't sit well with him. The frustration was the same as if he'd just blown a game-winning pass. "What kind of other things?"

"Yoga. Hair. Dancing." She laughed and held her hand out. "Anything, really. Everything. I want to do it all."

He eyed her hand. It was so small and dainty. He wanted to find the man who had held that hand, who had broken her heart and then let go of her, and tell him he was a fool. If he were any other man, if he actually wanted to be with someone in the way she deserved, he'd grab that hand right now and hold on as tightly as he could, and he'd never stop. Any man that was lucky enough to call her his should never let go.

Too bad that man couldn't be him.

Chapter Six

Wyatt Hamilton was in her living room, talking with her about things she normally had to buy a magazine to read about, and he seemed completely content to be doing so, and not even the slightest bit bored with her and her tiny home and sad stories about her ex and her inability to live her life to its fullest.

What was *happening*?

Who *was* she?

"I hope you get all those things," he said after a short period of silence. "You deserve them, and you deserve more than that man gave you."

She smiled. What did one say to that? She had no idea, so she settled for: "Thanks."

"Anytime." He drank his champagne, studying her living room. "Nice place you have here."

"Thanks." Ugh. She sounded like a broken record now. She tried to think of something witty to say, when all she could think was *Oh my God, Wyatt Hamilton's thigh is touching my knee!* She told herself to pull it together, and said, "You're so hot."

Well. That was a fail.

Way to go, Kassidy.

He choked on his drink, coughing.

She patted him on the back, unable to ignore how hard his muscles were under her fingers. She leaned in, wincing because she'd almost killed the star quarterback of her home team with her off the wall statement. "Sorry, too much?"

"No," he rasped. "I just...choked."

"Like you did with the Patriots last year?"

His jaw fell, and he placed a hand on his chest. "Ouch. That hurts, Kassidy. It really hurts."

"Sorry," she said, not really the least bit sorry. "I was mad you lost that game. I had a bet on it."

His eyes flashed with something that could only be described as heat. "You mean you actually bet on me sometimes?"

"Most of the time," she admitted.

"Nice to know." Slowly, he reached out and touched her cheek, but immediately pulled back. "I'll try not to let you down again."

She trembled, way too distracted by his touch to actually pay attention to his words at first. He'd touched her. *Why* had he touched her? "Uh...thanks."

Broken record time again.

"And..." He smiled and shifted back, putting more distance between them. "I think you're pretty hot, too."

"He says as he backs away from me," she muttered cheekily.

He laughed again. "Kassidy..."

"Sorry." She winced because she'd basically just called him out on lying about finding her attractive for the third time. What was wrong with her? Why hadn't he noticed she was a lost cause and left yet, just like her ex had? She refused to call him by his name. He didn't deserve it. He was like Voldemort. His name shall never be spoken. "I'm horrible at this."

He cocked his head. "At what?"

"Dating. Talking. Small talk."

He stiffened, and it was then that she realized she'd called this a date. She was an idiot. This wasn't, and never would be, a date. She'd told herself that enough times. "I mean, not that this is a date, it's not, but we're sitting here, having the type of conversations one has on a date, and you're hot, and you're looking at me with those bright blue eyes—like, seriously, how are they so pretty? It's not fair—and all I can think is that you're here with me, and you're so nice and cute and why can't I stop talking—?"

He pressed his finger to her lips, and she stopped talking immediately. His skin against her mouth was electrifying. There was no other way to describe it. "Shh. My turn."

She nodded, saying nothing.

To be honest, she was incapable of talking right now.

"This is as much of a date as anything else ever would be. I like you, Kassidy. I'm not gonna lie. You're gorgeous, and I'd like nothing more than to show you the best night of your life."

She licked her lips, her heartbeat picking up speed at that last part. "But...?"

"But I won't, and I'll tell you why." He set his glass down and took hers out of her hand before cupping her face with both hands. His skin on hers made her tremble. "If I did that, if I listened to my body and took you to your room and stripped that dress off you inch by inch, I would give you a night of pleasure. A night of sex. Then I'd walk away, and you'd never see me again because that's what I do. And you..." His grip on her shifted, and he moved imperceptibly closer to her despite his words. "You deserve more than that,

Kass."

She shivered, not so sure he was right. She would be perfectly content with a night in his arms, thank you very much. "But—"

"That doesn't mean I can't do this, though."

Without further warning, he closed the distance between them, taking his time so she could reject him if she wished. *As if.* His thumb on her lip had been electrifying, like a bolt of lightning, but his mouth on hers was a downright, full-blown thunderstorm. As his mouth moved over hers, he ran his thumb over her cheek, caressing her gently.

That small movement, that touch, was somehow more intimate than the kiss itself. It was like he cherished her, and cared for her, which was ridiculous because he barely even knew her. Man, he was good. *Too* good. She never wanted the kiss to end, but as with all good things, it did.

He pulled back, resting his forehead on hers.

"You're an amazing woman, Kassidy Thomas, and I wish nothing but the best for you." He shook his head slightly. "But I'm not it, so I refuse to allow myself to do anything more than appease my curiosity about what you taste like, and now that I found out…I'll never forget."

She hesitated, licking her lips. She could still taste him there on her mouth. "And what did I taste like?"

"Heaven. Pure heaven."

She sucked in a breath. "That's what I was going to say about you."

"Copycat," he teased, touching the tip of her nose playfully before pulling back to a more appropriate distance. She missed his touch immediately. "Thank you for everything."

She blinked. "Are you leaving?"

"I probably should, before I do something we both regret."

"I don't think I'd regret it," she mumbled under her

breath.

He smiled sadly and touched her chin. "You would, once I left."

"If you say so."

"I do." He leaned back on the cushions, his forehead wrinkling. "But that doesn't mean we can't spend the night together, without the mindless fucking."

Laughing, she gave herself a second by taking a quick, large gulp of liquid fortitude. "What, exactly, are you proposing?"

"I want to help you."

Her mind went to a dirty, dirty place. "Help me do what?"

"Live."

Yep. Now it was really there. "Live, how, exactly?"

"Well, I can't do everything for you or with you in one night—not to mention, I have no idea what you want to do to your hair or how to do it—but I happen to love yoga, and dancing, too."

She choked on her drink. "*Yoga*?"

"Absolutely. It's great for core strength."

"Let me get this straight," she said slowly. "You want to spend the night with me, not naked, but doing…yoga?"

"Or dancing."

"Dancing," she squeaked, repeating him again.

He nodded, taking her glass out of her hand for the second time that night. "Come on. Let's go."

"Right now?" she blurted out.

Catching her hand, he tugged her to her feet and didn't let go. "There's no time to waste."

"Why not?" she asked, confused.

"Because we might not be having sex, but my rule still applies. One night. One time, then I leave, and I don't come back." He touched her shoulder, skimming his fingers over her arm. She shivered, swaying closer. "I can't come back,

Kass."

"Why not?" She licked her lips. "I mean, if we're not...
you know...then what's the harm? If we're just friends, then
what's the worst that could happen?"

"I could want more," he admitted, his brow wrinkled as
he pulled her into his arms, one hand holding hers, the other
on her lower back. "With you, it would be easy to want more."

She hesitated, her hand on his biceps. "And that would
be so bad?"

"Yes," he said without a hint of doubt. "Ready?"

She nodded, a pang of pain shooting through her, which
made no sense at all. Why was she sad that Wyatt Hamilton
had admitted to finding her attractive, and that he could want
something with her? Maybe because he also said wanting her
would be *bad*. It wasn't too crazy that she was sad about that,
right? "Wait, we don't have music."

"I don't need any."

And then he swept her in a circle, moving around the
coffee table effortlessly and with a grace she'd only ever seen
him portray on the field. He moved with her in his arms like
he'd been made to dance instead of throw a ball, and that
only made him about a million times more attractive than
before.

"You take lessons?" she asked, breathlessly, as he twirled
her around her tiny home.

"Had to. My mom made me." He dipped her, holding
her close to his abs so she didn't fall. This was it. This was
where she wanted to die. Pressed against Wyatt Hamilton's
abs. "She said it would be as important as a well-rounded
education would be in the future."

He picked her back up, and she breathed quickly, her hair
flying at the sexy maneuver. "She was right."

"Maybe," he admitted. "You're a natural, too."

"I'm not so sure about that. I'm just following your lead."

He grinned, picking her up and spinning in a circle. She bent her legs in the air, mimicking what she'd seen on television automatically. "That's kind of how dancing works. It's a lot like sex, in that way."

She gasped, gripping his shoulders tightly. "What?"

"One partner takes the lead, the other follows."

She almost giggled but managed to hang on to her dignity by a small thread. "True," she managed to say without sounding like a schoolgirl. "That is how it works."

"Indeed," he said, his voice low as he set her down on her feet again.

"What else did your mother have you learn?" she asked to fill the silence.

His lips twitched. "How to set a place setting properly, the importance of a year on a good bottle of wine, ice skating, and pretty much everything you could possibly imagine."

"So, you were rich, then?"

"Yeah, you could say that," he admitted.

She nodded.

"You?" he asked after a short silence.

"Not rich. Never was."

"This house is perfect, though." He started moving again, sweeping her into her kitchen. "Mine's too big. I need to move."

She laughed. "I think it's perfect."

"Five bedrooms for one person, when I have no intention of ever adding on to that one person?" He snorted. "It's too much. I got too cocky when I started out, and I needed a big place to show my success. It was stupid, and I was young. A place like this, in the city, would be much better suited to my needs."

She nibbled on her lip, dying to ask him whether, if he fell in love with someone, he would walk away, but it was none of her business, really. After he left, the only time she'd see him would be on her television on Sunday afternoons.

"What's your biggest dream?"

"To dance with Wyatt Hamilton in my living room," she said immediately. "Oh…wait…guess I need a new dream."

He laughed shortly. "Yeah, you do."

"What's yours?"

"Uh-uh. That one doesn't count. I want the real one."

She hesitated. "I guess the opposite of you. Become financially stable. Pay off my house so I'm mortgage free, once I actually buy it—which I'm thinking of doing. I want to live my life, find someone who fits nicely in it, and start a family. Adopt a dog and a cat. Be…happy."

He said nothing at first, just tightened his grip on her hand, but then he said, "You rent now?"

"Yeah, but the owners want me to buy." She paused. "I'm considering it."

"Nice." He locked eyes with her. "I hope you get all those things you want."

"Me, too." She licked her lips, which were way too dry all of a sudden. "What is your biggest dream?"

"To be remembered for the rest of all time as one of the best quarterbacks ever," he immediately replied. "It's been my dream ever since I was old enough to throw a ball, and I doubt that'll ever change."

She rubbed his back as he danced, their movements slower with each step they took, until they were basically just holding one another and swaying slightly. "I think you'll get that, Wyatt. That, and more."

"I hope so," he murmured, his eyes still on hers. "Kassidy…"

Something charged the air, shooting off sparks, yanking them together bit by bit until there would be nothing left between them but bare skin and sweat. For a second, just one blissful second, he lowered his head, and she swore he was about to kiss her again…

Right until he let go of her, stepping back and dragging his hands down his face. "More champagne?" he asked, his voice slightly higher.

"Yes, please," she managed to say.

She was going to need it if she was going to survive the night…

With Wyatt Hamilton convinced he couldn't touch her.

Chapter Seven

Four hours later, they collapsed on her bed, breathing heavily. After they'd danced, they talked for a while, finishing off the bottle of champagne, and then he'd come up with the bright idea to try yoga. Only, it hadn't been such a bright idea, because every time she twisted and turned and fell, laughing, it had taken all his control not to crawl on top of her and kiss her until that laughter turned into groans and moans of pleasure. He couldn't touch her. She deserved more than a night in the arms of a playboy like him, one who could never be hers.

Still, against all logic, he wanted her more than anything. He wasn't satisfied with just this.

What the hell is going on with me?

Yawning, she rolled onto her side and smiled at him, her lipstick long gone, her hair sticking up everywhere. She was still, hands down, the most beautiful woman he'd ever seen, and he was, without doubt, enamored with her. He wasn't sure what to do about that.

What to say.

So, he said nothing at all.

She smiled sleepily at him and rubbed her nose. She was glowing ethereally. "Do you need something to change into? I mean, all I have is girl clothes, but you're welcome to use my pajamas. Warning, though. They're all gowns."

He frowned. "Gowns?"

"Yeah. Like…dresses."

He grinned up at her ceiling fan and rolled onto his back. Since they'd drunk way too much, they'd decided it would be a good idea for him to spend the night, and she had insisted he sleep in her king-size bed with her, since it was large enough for both of them—including him and his, as she called it, *big-ass muscles.* The fan whirled slowly, blowing a gentle breeze down on them. She shivered, so he sat up and tugged the comforter at the bottom of the bed over her body. "I'm good in this, thanks. If Anna found out I wore a gown, she'd tell the press."

She eyed his dress pants and partially unbuttoned shirt. "I wouldn't tell."

She was unbelievably adorable when she blushed like that. "I'm fine, it's not the first time I've crashed in my suit, and it won't be the last," he said.

"Don't you normally take them off, though?" She bit her lip. "With other girls you spend the night with but don't… *spend the night* with."

"Sometimes," he said idly. Reaching out, he played with a piece of her hair, tugging on it gently. "Sometimes not."

He didn't tell her she was the first woman he spent the night with that he hadn't slept with. This wasn't exactly chartered territory for him. It was bad enough she had a hold over him without knowing it. If he told her, there was no telling what would happen next. Being with her had been…fun. Yeah, that's right. *Fun.* He didn't really have fun anymore.

Instead, he focused on his game, on and off the field, and flitted from one chick to another, never stopping long enough to actually learn anything about them, for one very good reason…

So he couldn't fall for them.

But he'd broken his rule. He'd gotten close to a girl, and he liked what he saw. A lot. Now, there was nothing left to do but sober up and leave in the morning before he did something he regretted, like tell her how much he liked her. He didn't want to lead her on, to make her think he wanted more than a night of fun when he didn't.

And never would, no matter how much he liked her.

"How old's your sister?"

He let go of her hair. "She's probably about your age."

"Which is…?" she asked teasingly.

Shit. Didn't he read somewhere to never guess a woman's age? "I might not be a relationship guy, but even I'm smart enough to sense that this is a trap…"

"Fine, don't guess my age," she said, chuckling. "Tell me hers."

"Twenty-six." He flopped back again. "She's engaged."

"I'm twenty-four."

"Shit." He rolled toward her, smiling. "You're practically a baby."

"Hardly," she scoffed.

"When I was twenty-four, I was barely able to throw a ball."

"That's not true. You had great stats that year."

He blinked. "You memorized my stats?"

"Of course I did. I love football." She reached out and touched his cheek. "Tonight has been…surreal. Thank you for dancing with me, and teaching me yoga, and…"

Kissing her? Was that what she'd been about to say? He hoped not. If she thanked him for that, he might just have to do it again. "I agree. But it's not over yet." Unless she wanted it to be. Was that what she hinted at? "Or is that your polite way of kicking me out of your bed?"

"No, of course not." She bit her lip. He'd learned that she did that when she was thinking, or stressed about something. "You can stay all night if you want. I don't mind."

"Don't have to be in early for work?"

She smiled. "Nine. But that's not exactly early. You?"

"Practice at ten. Not early, either."

She tapped her fingers on the bed between them. "Are you nervous for this weekend?"

"Not really." He shrugged. "I don't really get nervous… like, ever."

She pressed her lips together. "*Ever*?"

"Correct," he said. "I've got to be the calm one out there. If I'm losing my shit and scared to lose, my team will sense it, and it messes up the whole vibe."

She locked eyes with him, her lips parted slightly. "But that's on the field. What about, like, real life? Dates? Interviews? Sex?"

"Sex doesn't make me nervous." He scooted closer to her, but then stopped himself. Bad. Fucking. Idea. "I know what I'm doing in bed, and as I said, it's like dancing. One partner takes the lead, and the other enjoys the ride, so to speak."

Her cheeks pinked even more, and her breath quickened. "Do you like to be in control, or do you like to enjoy the ride?"

Shit. He shouldn't answer that. But, in his defense, he hadn't started this topic. She had…and she deserved an answer, right? "I like to be in control. What about you?"

His voice sounded deeper than usual.

Fuuuuck.

"I…" She licked her lips, shifting slightly. "I guess I…I guess I'd like to enjoy the ride."

"You *guess*?" He frowned. "Are you...have you never...?"

"I have," she said quickly, passing pink and going straight to red at this point. "Just, only with one man, and not in five years."

"Jesus." He rolled onto his side so he could see her. Her mouth. Her eyes. Her slim, curvy body. Everything about her screamed perfection, and yet she'd kept herself locked away for five years because of an asshole who hadn't treated her right? That made him sad. "You need to get out there. I meant what I said earlier. You're the whole package. Some guy would be lucky to call you his."

She took a breath, her eyes glassing over with what might have been tears, but they disappeared when she blinked. "I'm going to. I'm going to live again."

"Good." Although, for some reason, the idea of her living through other men didn't sit well with him. In fact, he was pretty sure he was about to hurl. "You deserve happiness."

She bit her tongue. "So do you."

"I'm happy," he said, perhaps a little defensively.

He wasn't sure why, though.

"I'm going to remember this night, this conversation, fondly," she admitted. "I'll never forget that, for one night, I had a guy like you in my bed."

Unable to resist, despite the warning bells going off in his head, he pressed his mouth to her forehead, kissing her sweetly. Somehow, someway, it was even more personal than the kiss he had given her earlier in her living room. "Even when there's another man next to you?"

"I guess it depends on the guy, doesn't it?"

He closed his eyes, inhaling her scent. He should go as soon as the booze cleared from his mind, or maybe earlier, via Uber, but he didn't actually want to do so. Irrationally, it felt like once he left, his spot would immediately be filled with another man. He didn't want her alone and miserable, but the idea of her being in love with another man made him miserable.

What did that even *mean*?

He hadn't even fucked her, for Christ's sake.

She wasn't his. He didn't want anyone to be his.

And yet…

Obviously, she deserved every happiness in the world. She deserved a man who would stay by her side and love her, and show her she wasn't as boring as she liked to believe. Someone who would do yoga with her every night, and dance to no music, and wouldn't leave in the morning because he refused to jeopardize his career. He pulled back, cupping her cheeks but firmly reminding himself that she was not his for the taking. "Can I ask you for a favor?"

She blinked, holding on to his wrist. "Sure. Anything."

"Promise me you'll live? That you'll stop thinking you're boring and not worth getting to know? Because I can assure you, as a man who spent the night with you…you so are."

"I promise." She flicked her tongue over her lips. "You made it so easy to take that first leap of faith, to jump with both feet into new things, and I'm going to keep on doing it. Keep on jumping."

"No more being afraid?" he asked.

"No more being afraid." She rested a hand behind his neck. "Can you promise me something?"

"Yes."

"If you ever need anything—just a person to talk to, or a friend to do yoga with, someone to kiss without strings attached—call me. I'll be here, and I will never expect more out of you than you're willing to give me." She locked eyes with him. "*Never.*"

It would be so easy to take her up on that offer. To take what she was willing to give him, and give her nothing in return. It was what he did. Who he was. But with her…

He wanted to do better.

To *be* better.

An unfamiliar emotion swelled within him, choking him. He ached to pull her into her arms, whisper that she didn't need to date anyone else, that she could just fuck him, and then prove it to her through actions instead of words. He did none of those things. Instead, he said, "I promise."

With that, she smiled, closed her eyes, and moments later, she was asleep.

Just like that.

He watched her sleep for a little while, and his eyelids grew heavier with each breath she took. He wasn't sure how long he lay there, or when he'd fallen asleep too, but at some point, he must have, because when he opened his eyes, dawn was creeping over the sky and his head was clear of any lingering effects of alcohol, which meant...

It was time to go.

Turning his head slowly, he gazed at her beauty without her noticing. She had her hands folded under her cheek, and her eyes had drifted shut. Her chest rose and fell with each breath, and her cheeks had a rosy hue to them that he'd never forget. She was asleep next to him, wearing her dress from the night before, and he was also still fully clothed.

He didn't want to move.

Didn't want to stop holding her against him.

That was his cue to leave.

Still, he didn't move.

He glanced around the room. Light blue walls. Dresser topped with perfume, jewelry, and one family photo. A couple of romance books. A closet filled with clothes. A chair in front of a makeup mirror, with cups filled to the brim with brushes. Hair products were scattered over the top of the vanity, along with some makeup, too. All the things that he would assume a woman would have in her room were present, yet there was something special about it all. It was as if he saw into her life a little bit and understood her better.

Every shirt hanging in her open closet was prim. Proper. Pretty. Everything was put together with careful consideration. In its place. Properly organized. When she'd shown up on his doorstep and sung that song, she'd been begging for someone to take her out of her carefully constructed shell. She'd been dying to *live*.

She told him that he'd helped her find that thrill she'd so desperately needed. If that was true, then he could walk away from her happy. He'd helped her change her life.

He would have to be content with that.

It was all he could offer her.

Gritting his teeth, he rolled out of the bed, making sure to be silent as he walked over to her dresser where he'd seen a pen and a notepad. He could see the indent in the paper where she'd written something, and he touched it, tracing her elegant scrawl.

She had pretty writing. Much prettier than his.

Picking up the pen, he jotted down a quick message. After he finished, he tore the paper off, folded it in half, and placed it on the pillow where his head had been moments before.

After one last look at her rosy cheeks, parted lips, long lashes, and soft blond hair, he slipped out of her bedroom, grabbed his shoes off the floor, and walked out the door just like he'd said he would all along. And true to his word...

He didn't look back even once.

Chapter Eight

One week later, sweat rolled down Kassidy's cheek, and she held on tightly, putting every ounce of strength she had into thrusting her body forward. Her heart pounded fast, echoing in her ears, and she let out a groan as she pushed even harder, straining every muscle to get closer to her goal. Nothing happened.

"Son of a bitch," she snarled, kicking the hutch.

Howling, she clutched her toes and hopped in circles, shooting death glares at the offending piece of furniture the whole time. This morning, she'd woken up and decided her living room was boring and had the bright idea to change things up. Changing things up had gotten her a hutch that was stuck on a loose plank in the floor, and a throbbing toe.

Still, she didn't regret her choice.

Changing things up was a necessity in her new life.

Leaning against the wall, she closed her eyes and took a deep breath, still clutching her toe. Ever since Wyatt had stormed into her life and spent the night with her *without* sex, she'd been a different woman. She'd held true to her promise that she'd be better. Take chances.

A visit to the hairdresser had given her that strawberry blond she'd always wanted in her hair, and she'd mastered that spin class she'd been eyeing up for months. Yoga was now a favorite of hers at her gym, and on a whim, she'd even done some Zumba. Last night, when a friend she hadn't seen in three months invited her to dinner last minute, she'd said yes.

These things might be small, and to some they might even seem silly, but they were *changes*. And change was just what the doctor ordered.

Smiling, she remembered what his note had said.

Kass,

Tonight was incredible, and I'm glad I could help, in any small way, in your journey to shake things up. Make sure you take those chances. You deserve everything good in your life. You deserve to be happy. Never forget that—and I'll never forget my promise to you.

Wyatt

Well, she'd been doing her best to follow through with that, and she'd been doing a good job...up until the stupid hutch got stuck on the floorboard, anyway. Oh well. Guess it would stay there until she could con her brother into coming over and helping her. Not a huge deal. No big changes ever came easily, right? Opening her eyes, she pushed off the wall and headed to her phone. As she picked it up, she saw a notification from ESPN on the screen.

The name in the title made her breath catch in her throat.

The Savior's Wyatt Hamilton says he'll play this Sunday, despite recent injury and rumors that Coach Jeffries would have him sit out until playoffs.

Swiping over the notification, she skimmed the article, smiling when he was quoted to say, "I'd hate to mess up anyone's running bets, so if you're counting on me not playing this weekend, you'd better cancel those bets before it's too late. I'll be there, and my arm will be as strong as ever."

Chuckling, she couldn't help but wonder if that was a subtle hello to her.

Heck, she chose to believe it was, because she could. Even if it wasn't, she'd never find out, because it's not like he was calling her anytime soon to set the matter straight.

And she was fine with that. With never finding out if he was thinking about her, or if he remembered her as fondly as she did him.

Closing out the app, she opened up her texts with Caleb and fired one off: *I need help.*

What did you do now?

She typed back immediately, checking the time. *I was rearranging my living room, and the hutch got jammed on a floorboard. I can't move it, no matter how hard I push.*

Ugh. Fine. I'll be by in two hours. Followed by: *But you'll owe me pizza and beer.*

She bit her lip. *I can't do two hours from now.*

Why not?

Should she tell him the truth? *I have a date.*

WITH WHO?

No one you would know.

Heck, she'd never even met the dude. She'd matched with him on eHarmony. All she knew was he was twenty-seven, an accountant like her, and he wore a suit well, if his profile pic was to be believed. She'd never gone a date with a stranger before, especially not someone she met on the internet, but it was all part of her change.

What's his name? How'd you meet? What does he do for

a living?

Rolling her eyes, she started to type back a reply telling him it was none of his frigging business, but then her doorbell rang. Frowning, she set the phone down and made her way to the door. She wasn't expecting anyone, and her friends weren't really the "stop by unannounced" type, so she couldn't imagine who might be here.

Unless…

It was *Caleb*.

If he'd zoomed over here from his place down the street simply because she'd mentioned having a date later, he'd taken the overbearing brother role to a *whole* new level. Pushing her glasses into place, she swung the door open, expecting to see her annoying brother standing there…and instead got the surprise of her life.

Wyatt Hamilton.

On her doorstep.

Not speaking, she tried to figure it out. Why was he here? What did he want? Had he forgotten something? Was he lost? In danger? Escaping paparazzi? She craned her neck, glancing behind him, but there were no cameras and no signs of danger chasing him.

When she remained silent, he lifted a hand, smiling that same devastatingly charming smile that had haunted her in her dreams and her bed for the past three nights. "Hey, Kass."

"Uh…" She desperately smoothed her horribly messy hair. It was useless. She hadn't been expecting company, and it showed. God, it showed. "Hi?"

That smile that widened. "Is that a question?"

"Um, yes?" She laughed a little. "Not to be rude, but what are you doing here? Did you forget something? I mean, I didn't see anything, but you're free to check—"

"I didn't forget anything," he said, studying her with a slight frown. "But you told me if I ever wanted someone to hang out with, to spend time with…"

"Oh. *Oh*. Right."

Holy crap, he was actually taking her up on that offer?

He hesitated. "Am I interrupting something?"

"Huh? No." She pursed her lips. "Why?"

He rubbed his hard jaw. He had a bit of a five o'clock shadow going, and his dark blond hair was sticking up like he'd been running his fingers through it. He wore a Saviors T-shirt that hugged his biceps and chest, a pair of black sweats that hugged other things, aviator sunglasses, and a pair of Nikes. Sweats had never been so sexy before. "You're all sweaty. Is someone here with you? I can go…"

"Oh. That." She glanced at herself. She, too, was wearing sweats, but not nearly so sexily. Sexy? Sexy-ish? What the heck was the word? Oh, who *cared* anyway? Wyatt Hamilton was here, on her doorstep, with hungry eyes. "No. I'm all alone. What about you? Are you alone?"

What a stupid question.

She could *see* he was alone.

Good one. Way to charm him.

"Yeah, I'm alone." He rubbed the back of his neck. "I just left practice. I was driving home, and realized how close I was to you, so I figured I'd stop by and see how you were doing on that promise you made me."

Funny, he hadn't mentioned he'd be stopping by in his letter to her. Actually, that letter had seemed like a pretty solid good-bye to her. "Oh, well, I…uh…" She laughed nervously. "I'm good."

"Good," he said, shifting his weight to his left foot.

"How are you?" she added hastily.

"Good. Good." He shoved his hands in his pockets and rocked back on his heels. "Just the usual. Sleep. Protein. Practice. You know."

She nodded, even though she didn't. "Yeah. Sure."

They both fell silent.

After a while, he cleared his throat.

The awkwardness between them was tangible enough to bottle and sell. "Did you, uh, have a good practice?"

"Yeah, it was a tough one, but we needed that to be ready for the Giants. We had double practice time all week long."

"Ugh," she muttered. Last time the teams had played one another, the Saviors had lost by fifteen points. "You're playing, right?"

"Yeah." He rotated his shoulder. He'd injured it a few weeks ago when DeMarquez had taken him down too hard. "I'm fine. They worry too much."

"You seemed fine last week," she said under her breath, heat flushing through her as she remembered all the ways he'd lifted, twisted, and turned during yoga.

He laughed. "Better than fine, even."

"Well…" They locked eyes. "I'd hope so."

"Have you been keeping your promises?" He rocked back on his heels again. "Living life to its fullest, and taking chances?"

"I have." She gestured down at herself. "Hence the sweatiness."

"What were you doing?" he asked curiously.

She rested her shoulder on the doorjamb. "I decided to change the layout of my living room for the first time since moving in here."

"Wow. Crazy," he said wryly. "We might need to talk about toning it back a little bit. You're taking this whole living life to its fullest thing a little too far."

She smacked his arm playfully. "Hey, considering I measured each piece and placed it perfectly in position five years ago, it *is* crazy. For me, anyway."

"I'm kidding." He gave her a half smile. It was the sexiest thing she'd ever seen before. "Can I see it?"

"What?" She glanced over her shoulder. "My living room?"

"Yeah."

She bit her lip. "Why would you want to see my rearranged living room?"

"Why not? I can think of worse ways for a guy like me to spend my afternoon." He laughed uneasily and dragged a hand through his hair. "In case you couldn't tell by my awkwardness earlier, I don't know what I'm doing here, or why I'm here, but I am because I couldn't keep driving. That might be bad, or it might be good, but whatever the hell it is, I want to see you, so I'm here. Seeing you. Because I missed you, Kass. And I never miss anyone."

He missed her. She held her breath, a million things racing through her mind, but she couldn't catch a single one. The thoughts were too fast. Too fleeting. Too... "In that case, would you like to come in and see my messy living room?"

He laughed. Short. Hard. "Yes, I'd like to see your living room."

"Then, please, come inside."

She stepped back, and he brushed past her, a whiff of cologne and sunshine teasing her senses. His smell was somehow familiar and comforting, even though she'd only smelled it one other time. Of course, that had been the best night of her life, so maybe that made sense. Maybe that's why smelling him made her let out a sigh of relief that she'd been holding in for three days.

It certainly wasn't relief that he'd come back to her.

This meant nothing. *They* meant nothing.

And she'd best remember that.

Chapter Nine

Clearly, Wyatt had no clue what the hell he was doing anymore. He'd been fine. He'd been great. He'd been at practice, doing his own thing, not missing anyone or anything at all, but the second he pulled out of the parking lot, he'd gone back to the place he'd been every second of every day since the moment he walked away from Kassidy Thomas—he'd been in his head, with her, wanting her, missing her.

She was all he could think about.

All he *dreamed* about.

Hell, he even swore he smelled her every time he woke up in the morning, but when he opened his eyes…she, of course, was never there. She was just a memory of a night he'd shared with a woman that he couldn't forget, and he wasn't sure what to do about that.

He'd never wanted more than one night.

Never ached for a woman so badly it messed with his head.

So, as he'd been driving home to crash on his couch with a beer and some old Giants games he planned to binge on so he could study Manning, he'd been unable to ignore the fact that there might be a glaring solution to his little problem: he just needed to see her again.

One more night with her. One more time sharing secrets and laughs.

Then he'd be healed of the hold she had over him.

There was no other answer to his dilemma.

"I can't wait to see…" As he walked into her house, he faded off. The weight he'd been carrying on his shoulders since the moment he'd left her sleeping alone in her bed lifted, and he smiled when he caught sight of her living room. Furniture was pushed away from all the walls haphazardly, and there was no rhyme or reason. Her living room looked like it had been arranged by a blindfolded three-year-old. "It's, uh"—he rubbed his jaw and laughed—"great."

She rolled her eyes at him again. He'd never found eye-rolling so adorable until he met her. "This isn't how I'm leaving it."

"Good. Because *this* isn't living your life to its fullest."

A laugh-snort escaped her. "I wanted this," she touched the hutch in the middle of the living room, then went to a bare spot on the wall. "to be over here, but it got stuck."

He walked around it, rubbing his chin. "I see that. Want some help?"

"I asked Caleb to help me," she said, her cheeks flushing pink as she adjusted her red-rimmed glasses. "He said he'd be by later to do it."

"Well, I'm here now, so why wait for him when you don't have to?" He went behind the furniture, tugged it back effortlessly from the planks where it had been wedged, then started pushing it to where she stood. "Watch out, short stuff."

She bolted out of the way, her eyes wide. "How are you moving that so easily?"

"Lots of weight lifting and throwing balls around." He

pushed it where she wanted it to go and wiped off his hands. "This is nothing."

"I see that," she said, avoiding his eyes. "All those muscles at work again."

"You're kind of obsessed with my muscles," he teased.

She blinked. "Well, can you blame me? I mean, look at them."

He laughed, saying nothing.

As he moved the furniture, a random thought popped into his head. "Did your ex ever live here with you?"

"N-No." She hugged herself. "Why?"

"Just wondering." For some reason, the idea of that man being in this house with her annoyed him. Inexplicably, he wanted to be the only man here. "What did he do for a living?"

"He didn't. He was in school. Still is in law school, last I heard." She crossed her arms. "He used to dream of being on the Supreme Court. It was part of our plan. First graduation. Then marriage. Then kids. Then the world. He had no doubt he'd be able to get there, too. He had connections."

Wyatt rolled his eyes. "Yet another entitled asshole."

"Pretty much," she said.

"My brother is a lawyer."

"I'm sorry," she immediately said.

He laughed. "Nah, he's not too bad. He lives in a small town and mostly works with business owners and old people."

"Is that Eric? The one who moved for a girl?"

"Yes," he said, impressed she remembered that. "What's next?"

"Huh?"

He pointed at the couch that was diagonal and blocking the entrance to the kitchen. "Want me to move that, or do you like it there?"

"Oh, uh, yeah, sure." She stepped aside and crinkled her

nose. "Over there, under the window, please?"

Without replying, he moved her couch where she wanted it. He stopped at the table that had been behind the couch and cocked an eyebrow. "What about this?"

She pointed, and he picked it up, since it was light, setting it into place. When he turned back around to face her, her mouth was parted and her eyes slightly glossy as she focused on his arms. His response was immediate, and he took a step toward her without realizing it.

Letting out a small breath, she cleared her throat. "Uh, all that's left is that loveseat."

He glanced at the object in question, his pants a hell of a lot tighter than they'd been moments before because he was picturing exactly what he'd like to do to her on that loveseat.

Damn it.

He took another step closer to her, but then made himself stop. Nothing had changed. He still couldn't give her a relationship, and still wasn't willing to jeopardize his career over a woman. But she'd sworn to him she would never ask him for more than he was willing to give, and he knew exactly what she meant by that. If he took her up on her offer, she would give herself to him, and ask for nothing in return. She would be *his*.

"Where's it going?" he asked, walking over to it, his voice thick.

She pointed. Her finger trembled slightly. "There."

Bending over, he moved the loveseat easily. Her eyes were on him the whole time, and he'd swear she did more than look. He'd been with a lot of women, liked a lot of women, but he'd never been so attuned to a person that he could tell they were watching him. But with her, he could.

What did that *mean*?

"Thank you," she said quietly.

"You're welcome." He rubbed his chin and surveyed his

handiwork. The couch was slightly off center. He walked over to it, pushed it, and then nodded. "There. Perfect."

"Yeah, it is," she said immediately.

Something told him she wasn't talking about the couch.

"Do you want something? Coffee? A beer? Water?" She jerkily shoved her hair behind her ears. "I mean, it's the least I can do for your help."

"Hmm." He walked toward her slowly, watching her as he drew closer. She sucked in a deep breath and lifted a foot, but didn't back up. "I'd love a beer."

"Sure." She headed into the kitchen, and he followed her. They passed a framed picture with her, her brother, and her parents in it. She was smiling, but it didn't seem real. She opened the fridge, bent over, and pulled out a Budweiser. "Thank you, by the way."

"You're welcome," he said from directly behind her.

She gasped and turned around, glancing up at him. She was only a couple of inches away. That was a couple of inches too many, to his thinking. His heart pounded against his ribs, and even though he should keep his hands to himself, he reached out to touch her cheek. It was as soft as he remembered. He'd missed her.

Everything about her.

Trembling, she held out the cold beer. "Here you go."

"Thanks." He twisted the lid off and tossed it on the counter. "Are you joining me to celebrate the finished job?"

She shook her head, not backing up, but not moving closer, either. Her gaze fell to his jaw, oddly enough, and she swallowed hard. "No, thank you. But if I can ever repay the favor somehow…"

"Actually, now that you mention it?" He took a swallow of the beer, letting it roll down his throat and cool him off a bit. Around her, he was always too hot.

She rubbed her arms. "Yeah?" she asked, her voice

breathy.

"About that favor," he said, stepping closer, not touching her, but towering over her. "I have to go to dinner with a guy who retired from the game thirty years ago, and as much as I like and admire the dude, he has a tendency to babble on and on about all his glories in the good old days, and how the game isn't as good anymore."

She sucked in a breath and swayed closer. "Okay…"

"So, to be honest." His fingers brushed the smooth plastic of her glasses as he tucked her hair behind her ear. It was as soft as he remembered. "I could really use a wingman. Someone who can loudly announce we have somewhere else to be when I nudge them under the table discreetly, and then we get out of there at a decent time."

She nodded. "Okay, yeah, sure. I'm your girl. When is it?"

"Tonight, in two hours." He'd been planning on making excuses to get out of it, citing the big game this weekend as an excuse, but now… "Are you free?"

After licking her lips, she shook her head, nodded, then shook her head again. "I, well, I kind of had plans."

He cocked his head and moved a fraction of an inch closer. Her nostrils flared in response. "What kind of plans?"

"Well, you see, I've never tried online dating before. I've always been too nervous to meet some dude I've never even seen, and to just blindly trust the internet to know what I might like in a guy." She licked her lips. "So, when I matched with this guy on eHarmony right away, and he messaged me…I didn't ask questions. I just said yes when he asked me out. He seemed funny enough, and he didn't talk like a serial killer, so, long story short, we're supposed to go out later today."

"How do serial killers talk?" he interjected.

"I have no clue." She made a stabbing motion with her

hand, holding an imaginary knife. "Like, sharp?"

He cracked up, holding his stomach, bending over.

"*Anyway.* I let him pick the place. Otherwise I'd have to figure out the perfect spot, and it would take forever, and then I'd back out, and probably say something came up, like the old me would have, and—"

He straightened at that, his laughter dying. "Where did he pick? You can tell a lot about a guy from the place he chooses for a first date," he stated, trying to ignore the uneasiness in the pit of his stomach at the idea of her going out with some other dude instead of him. Maybe this dude would have sex with her, instead of respecting her enough to wait. Maybe he would stick around longer than a night. Maybe she would fall in love with him. Get married. Have adorable kids. Live happily ever after.

He was going to hurl.

"Costello's."

He winced and brushed a strand off her cheek, burying his fingers in the hair on the back of her head. There was no way he was going to stand by and watch her fall in love with some other guy while they had this...this...tension between them. "Sounds like a serial killer restaurant to me. If they have sharp knives, don't walk. Don't stop. Don't pass go. *Run.*"

She half laughed, half groaned, her lids drifting shut. Her lashes were unadorned with mascara, yet they were the longest he'd ever seen. She ran her hands down his shoulders gently, making his body tense and flex with the undeniable need to have her. "You think he's a killer?"

"Oh, he's definitely a killer." He pressed his lower body against hers, showing her just how badly he wanted her. Hell, she'd touched him, so he got to touch her, too. And she'd made him promise... "You're risking total dismemberment if you go out with him."

She didn't say anything. Just gripped his biceps, digging her nails into his skin. Lifting her chin, she licked her lips and locked eyes with him, smiling slightly. "So, what should I do?"

"If it were me, and I had to choose between a serial killer and a peaceful dinner with a guy I knew wasn't going to kill me…" He slipped his fingers under her chin, lifting it and lowering his head until his mouth was a breath away from hers. "Why bother with a blind date from hell, when you could spend the night with me instead?"

"Why indeed?" she said cheekily.

"Hey. Did you mean what you said when you said if I wanted to come back…?" he started to ask.

She nodded, a small whimper escaping her. "Yes."

"That you wouldn't ask me for more than I could give?"

She nodded again.

"Because I can't stop thinking about you. About how right your body pressed against mine is, and how badly I want to find out how good you taste everywhere."

Trembling, she swayed closer. "I've been thinking about that, too. And you."

"But the thing is, I respect you, and more than that, I *like* you."

"Same."

"I can't offer you love, or forever. I couldn't even say if I'd be back after tonight or not. You deserve more than that." His grip on her shifted, and his hand slid lower. "But the idea of you going on a date with someone else…I don't like it."

"Then I won't do it," she said breathlessly. "I don't even know the guy."

He shook his head, trying to talk himself out of this, as well as her. "But I can't offer you any—"

"You know, you're probably right about the serial killer thing, and I enjoy being with you, so…" She wrapped her arms around his neck and rose on tiptoe. "It's cool. I'll cancel to help you out."

"Are you sure?" He caressed her cheek tenderly, seconds from giving in and taking what she offered because there was no way he was walking away from her twice.

"I've never been more sure of anything in my life," she said, her voice breathy. "Kiss me, Wyatt Hamilton."

He groaned and lifted her onto the counter and stepped between her thighs, pressing against her intimately. She sucked in a deep breath and closed her eyes...so he kissed her.

And, in that moment, everything was right again.

Chapter Ten

Kassidy tightened her fists on his shirt, all doubts and breath leaving her the second his mouth touched hers. Part of her was convinced this was another dream, and the other part was all too aware of how very real this was. With his hands on her, and his thighs between hers, there was no imagining how right this felt. She'd tried.

But her dreams always ended up falling short of perfection.

He ran his hands up her thighs, stopping an inch from where she ached for him most, and kissed her like the world might end if he didn't. And for a second, she thought it had, as his tongue slipped between her lips, touching hers. The room around them started to spin. He'd knocked her off her feet last time, but this time was proving to be even more amazing than before, and they'd just started.

That hadn't seemed possible.

Arching her back to get closer to him, she squeezed him with her thighs, needing more. Needing *him*. He seemed to understand what she wanted without her having to say the words. He removed her leggings with surprisingly little effort, considering the fact she was sitting on the counter. Her shirt went next, and soon enough she wore nothing more than a pair of panties, while he was still fully clothed. She shivered, lifting her arms to cover herself, oddly vulnerable until he stepped back, his heated eyes skimming her body.

Flexing his jaw, he stepped back between her thighs, resting his hands on her bare skin. "Even better than I imagined."

Shivering for a different reason, she said, "Wyatt, I—*oh my God*."

He kissed her neck, leaving a trail of fire in his wake as his hands slid upward toward her core. When his fingers brushed her intimately, she gasped again, clinging to him desperately. He'd barely even done anything, and yet she was already madly frantic for him to do more.

To make her his for the day.

"Wyatt," she breathed, biting her lip as he bit her shoulder.

He moved lower, over the curve of her bare breast. "Yeah?"

"Why do you still have all your clothes on?"

With a small laugh, he whispered: "Patience, my dear. Patience."

Then he closed his mouth over her hard nipple. He sucked the bud into his mouth, swirling his tongue over her. She threaded her hands through his hair and moaned, closing her eyes slightly. "But—"

"If I undress, nothing will stop me from having you." His gaze collided with hers, and he moved to her other nipple. "I want to take my time with you. Make you scream. Taste you…everywhere."

She licked her lips. "Everywhere?"

"Everywhere." He smirked. It was the sexiest smirk she'd ever seen. "Then, and only then, I'll undress and let you have a turn."

With that, he took her other nipple into his mouth, giving it the same treatment as the first. She let his mouth take her on a ride, losing herself in the slow stroke of his tongue. When he released her nipple and kissed lower, and lower still, she stiffened. Her ex had never…he hadn't liked…but would *she*?

He'd dropped to his knees, bringing his face level with— well, with *her*. He nibbled on the spot right above her knee, then went higher, dropping a kiss midway up her thigh. One more had him right below her panties. He paused, studying her. "Are you okay—?"

She nodded, biting her lip in anticipation. "Go ahead."

Without hesitation, he lowered his mouth to her core, rolling his tongue over the thin satin of her panties. Moaning, she threaded her hands in his hair, urging him closer.

Oh, yeah. She *liked*.

His tongue brushed over her relentlessly, driving her higher and higher until she was moving against him erotically, everything else lost in her mind except for her need to come. And when she did orgasm, she flew higher than ever before, and he was right there to pull her safely back to the ground again.

Standing back up, he pressed his mouth to hers as he undid his pants. He set a condom on the counter before he let them hit the floor. He broke off the kiss long enough to pull his shirt over his head, and then he was back on her, running his hands down her back smoothly. When his hands closed over her breasts, she gasped into his mouth, rocking against his erection wantonly and letting him take control like he'd said he liked to do. Every nerve in her body was still alive and humming, and the pressure of him against her was almost enough to send her over the edge again. So, she kept doing it. Moving against him.

Pleasure shot through her, making her move more

impatiently.

More rushed.

He groaned into her mouth and thrust against her. Pleasure rocketed through her, and she dug her nails into his shoulders before letting herself explore the inches of bare skin he'd given her when he'd removed his clothes. He was as hard as she remembered, if not harder, and every inch of skin she touched was more addictive than the last.

He groaned, kissing her and pulling back. "I missed you so much."

"I missed you, too."

He caught her hands, holding them firmly. "You don't understand what that means. I want you to understand that you're special to me. That this…"

She nodded, her heart picking up speed. "I know."

Slowly, she ran her fingers down his back, then around his waist and down between them. When she closed her hand over his huge erection, he froze and drew in a ragged breath. She jerked on him, and he kissed her again, more frantically this time. When she continued moving her hand over him, trying to bring him as high as he'd brought her, he grabbed her wrist and held on tight. "*Enough.*"

She shook her head. "Not enough. Not even close to enough."

"You're right, it's not enough," he growled.

As he ripped open a condom packet, he locked eyes with her as he rolled it into place, pinching the tip. He mesmerized her. Hard abs. Harder erection. Heated eyes. Messy light brown hair. "And that scares the shit out of me."

She blinked, confused.

Was he implying…?

Before she could ask questions, he stepped between her legs, lifted her hips slightly, shoved her panties to the side, kissed her passionately, and thrust inside of her.

At *last*, he was inside her.

And it was incredible.

Crying out into his mouth, she wrapped her legs around his bare hips as tightly as she could and held on for dear life. He moved inside of her, bringing her higher with each thrust of his hips until she was sure she couldn't go any higher without dying.

But then she did, and she didn't die, but still went to heaven.

Every nerve, every muscle, tightened in awareness as he thrust inside her, harder and smoother with each stroke he made. Each movement was like taking a step up a staircase, until she was at the top, trembling and calling his name wildly, and then *bam*. She couldn't see anything but pleasure bursting into flares of light.

And he was right there with her, calling her name.

He dropped his forehead to the cabinet beside her head, groaning, and she clung to him, half on the counter, half off of it, the world slowly coming into focus again despite the fact that her glasses were crooked and hanging off her left ear, and he was still buried deep inside her.

She'd just had sex with Wyatt Hamilton.

Letting out a soft laugh, he positioned her more firmly on the counter and pulled back, meeting her eyes. Smiling, he pushed her glasses back into place, that tender moment sending a pang of something almost painful through her chest. "That was...wow."

Biting down on her lip, she smoothed his hair off his forehead. "Yeah."

He smiled and withdrew from her body, and it took all her control not to grab on to him and pull him right back where he'd been. "Are you okay? I wasn't too rough with you, right?"

"Not at all."

"Good." He kissed her again, his mouth lingering over hers. "So. What do you say? Want to go to this dinner with me?"

As if he even had to ask. Honestly, he could ask her to go to hell for him, and she'd probably say yes, as long as he asked her after making her visit heaven first. "I'd love to go to dinner with you."

"Excellent." He grinned. It was, hands down, the sexiest grin she'd ever seen in her life, and she'd never forget it. Not in a million years. Her heart picked up speed as he gripped his cock, peeling the condom off carefully. "Do you have a downstairs bathroom?"

"Yes. Down the hall, to your left," she called out.

While he cleaned up in there, she washed her hands, freshened up with paper towels, and quickly redressed. It was one thing to be naked in her kitchen while having sex, but it was quite another to stand there in the light of day, all alone in nothing more than her black underwear. If Mrs. Corgin saw her through the window, she might just have another heart attack.

As she tugged her shirt down, Wyatt came walking back into the kitchen, butt naked and clearly not caring about it. He took one look at her clothed form and frowned. "Too many clothes."

She snorted. "Sorry, I'm not walking around naked all day."

"And why not?" he shot back.

"Because I'm not *that* adventurous."

"That's a shame," he said, stepping into boxers. "You've got the body to be a nudist."

She laughed, saying nothing.

Honestly, she had nothing to say.

"So how am I doing?"

"Huh?" she asked.

"Are you living right now?"

She cocked her head, watching him step into his pants. "Is that what you're doing? Making me live?"

"Maybe," he said, winking.

"And here I was thinking you moved furniture for me out of the goodness of your heart."

"That, too," he said, grinning crookedly.

"Well, either way, I'd say you're doing very well." She wrapped her arms around herself, her attention on those abs of his. She'd never been much of an abs girl, but for him? She totally was. "I'm alive right now."

"Good." He came over to her and pulled her into his arms. "Now that you mention it, so am I."

"Weren't you already living life to its fullest?" she asked a bit sarcastically. "I've seen the news about you. You're hardly living the life of a hermit."

"That might be true, but I guess I'm learning there's a difference between having fun with someone for a few hours, and learning to enjoy someone's company on a different level." He skimmed the backs of his knuckles down her cheek, swallowing hard. "With you, I find myself acting a little more...*free*. More like myself."

She tucked her messy hair behind her ear, her heart skipping a beat. "I get what you mean. I'm myself, too, with you."

"The question is," he curled his hand behind the nape of her neck. "What the hell does it all mean?"

"I don't know," she answered honestly.

"Yeah. Me, either."

They remained silent, both studying each other.

She couldn't help but think that he was measuring her, trying to figure out her weaknesses, and part of her wanted to hide them from him—while the other half wanted him to see them all.

It was frightening…and confusing.

"What's your favorite meal?" he asked, breaking the silence.

"Uh…" She laughed a little uneasily. "Homemade chicken parm, I guess. It has to be pounded really thin, and then fried, and then baked with sauce and mozzarella cheese. I make it, and to be honest, I've never had any at a restaurant that is better than mine. It's a science to get the sauce to cheese ratio right, and you need to match it to the thickness of the chicken. It's gotta be just right."

He nodded, looking far too serious for such an unimportant question. "That sounds delicious."

"It is." She tightened her grip on his shoulders—which she'd forgotten she was holding on to until now. "If you win against the Giants, I can make it for you."

He turned his head to the side. "And if I lose?"

"What's your favorite meal?"

"Grilled steak, marinated onions, and mashed potatoes," he answered immediately.

"Then you have to make me that," she said, biting her lip as soon as the words came out of her mouth. Was it too much? Too forward of her to assume he might want to see her again after tonight was over and she'd returned the favor due him? Yep. It was definitely too much. *Fool.* "Never—"

He laughed and rubbed his jaw. "Deal."

"If you're sure," she said quickly.

"I'm sure." He stepped back, nostrils flaring, and let go of her. "Nothing wrong with a healthy little bet between friends, right?"

"Is that what we are?" she asked breathlessly. "Friends?"

He nodded once. "I'd like to be, yes. I can't ask for more than that, though, because—"

"You don't want a relationship," she finished for him, smiling when he flushed. "You don't have to keep telling me.

I swear not to fall in love with you, and I swear not to read too much into us hanging out every once in a while."

"Good. And I swear the same." He held a hand up solemnly. "Here and now, I also swear not to fall for you, or to read into things intentions that aren't there."

She chuckled. "Then it's settled. We have a deal."

Holding a hand out, he asked, "Should we shake on it?"

They were shaking on their agreement not to fall for one another more so than they were their little dinner arrangement. She had basically just agreed to a friends-with-benefits situation, something she'd never embarked upon before, but that was just fine with her. If she got to spend more time with Wyatt Hamilton, she'd take it, no matter what he wanted to call it. "Sure."

Sliding her hand into his, she shook it firmly and started to let go. He tightened his grip and pulled her into his arms, kissing her until she lost track of time and any silent agreements. When he pulled back, she clung to him breathlessly, blinking up at his blurry face.

"Sorry. I prefer kissing on agreements," he said, his tone low and rumbly.

It was sexy as hell.

"Noted," she said breathlessly.

He swung her back to her feet, letting go. "Speaking of kissing, you can still date around and live your life. Because we're just...friends. Like I said, I don't like the idea of you with another guy, but I also have no right to ask you not to see other men when I'm not giving you more than this," he said gently, tucking her hair behind her ear, his jaw tighter than usual. "Don't let me stop you, is all I'm saying."

She didn't say anything.

Just nodded.

He stepped back. "I'm going to run home, shower, and get changed. I'll pick you up at seven, okay?"

"Sure," she said. "What should I wear?"

"Any dress you'd like. It's casual."

She nodded. "O-okay."

As he walked out of her kitchen, he bent and swooped up his shirt and shoes on the way. "And Kass?"

"Yeah?" she asked, admiring his butt as he bent, because it was a fine butt.

"Just a fun little tip," he said, winking. "You've never lived until you've gone out in public without a pair of underwear on. You should try it sometime."

She choked on a laugh. "Will you be forgoing them tonight?"

"Maybe. Maybe not."

Before she could reply, he was gone, pulling his shirt over his head as he disappeared.

Chapter Eleven

All night long, she'd been on his mind. Even though she was right next to him, holding his hand or his arm all night, speaking to him, all he could think about was getting her home and getting her all to himself again. She was beautiful. Funny. Smart. Charming. He couldn't get enough of her. To be honest, he was starting to worry he never would.

She wore a black dress that hugged her curves. The dress came together with a bow on her stomach, and she'd matched it with a pair of lacy black high heels.

He kept getting distracted by that bow, fantasizing about undoing it like he was unwrapping the prettiest present he'd ever received. Had she skipped the underwear like he'd teasingly suggested? If he tugged on that bow and let the dress hit the floor, would she be naked? Would goose bumps rise over her flesh, her thighs trembling as she waited for him to make his next move, her cheeks flushed and her lips parted on a breath?

The mere image in his head was enough to make his pants grow tighter.

Jesus. What the *hell* was wrong with him?

She glanced at him, a glass of wine in her hand as she smiled at something George Waverly said. He'd been talking about how many yards he'd scored in the Super Bowl back in the late nineties, and Kassidy, bless her, had been listening intently the whole time, hanging on every word the gray-haired man said. She actually seemed interested in Waverly's endless stories about football.

Even more so than *he* was.

And he *loved* football. It was his *life*.

He'd never been with a girl who actually enjoyed football talk. Throughout dinner, she'd quoted a few stats that he knew for a fact were correct, showing an impressive knowledge about the game he loved more than life itself. It was sexy as hell, and when she told Waverly she remembered the score of that Super Bowl—correctly—it took every ounce of his self-control not to stand up, tell Waverly good-bye, and carry her out of the restaurant over his shoulder.

He needed her all to himself.

She could talk dirty to him all night about football, and stats, and plays, and he'd make her scream his name in return. Her laugh broke into his thoughts, and he ripped himself out of his fantasies. "Yeah, but he's got time," she said.

Who had time?

"Still—" Waverly started.

"He's only five years into his NFL career, and he's already been one of the highest scoring quarterbacks these past few years. Last year alone, he almost defeated Brady for most yards covered."

Wait. Was she talking about him?

"Last week alone, he covered four hundred and twenty yards."

She'd told him the other night she knew his numbers, but he'd figured that she was just trying to impress him. But she hadn't been full of shit after all.

She was an enigma, his Kassidy.

He was going to keep her up all night, and he had every intention of asking everything and anything about her that popped into his head. He wanted to learn it all.

Waverly scoffed. "And you think he can beat Brady's record?"

Kassidy nodded.

"Hmph." He gestured to Wyatt. "I like ya and all, kid, but not even *I* am willing to go that far."

"You should be." She pointed at him. "Last year..." She proceeded to rattle off every stat the NFL had put out on him, with precision and perfection.

His jaw hung open.

Where had she *been* his whole life?

Had he been wrong to avoid befriending her? Could he have her and not sacrifice his game? Or had she come along as a temptation, one he was supposed to overcome to prove his commitment to his career?

Shit if he knew.

She'd turned his world over onto its side, and he was still trying to figure out which way was up and which was down.

"Would you care to put your money where your mouth is?" Waverly asked her, smirking and leaning back in his chair.

"I would. Within the next five years, he will beat Brady."

Waverly held his hand out. "The stakes?"

"Box seats at the playoffs."

The older man laughed. "No messing around, huh?"

"I want to be there to see him win," she said, shrugging.

Wyatt cleared his throat. "Kass, Waverly never loses a bet."

"I don't care. Your precision is better than Brady's, and I have every belief that, given time, you'll beat him. I'm confident in my wager."

The way her eyes lit up with excitement as she spoke, like she couldn't wait to see it happen? Yeah, it did shit to him. Shit that he took no responsibility for...nor for the actions that followed.

Unable to resist, he reached across the distance between them, curled his hand behind her neck, and kissed her, right there in front of everyone. She gasped but then melted against him, opening her lips.

He pulled back without taking advantage of that offer and pressed his mouth to her ear. "Hearing you talk stats like that is even hotter than you arguing on my behalf for more money. You're so sexy."

Her grip on her glass tightened. "Oh yeah?"

"Yeah."

"I feel the same way about you," she breathed.

Waverly cleared his throat. "Well, it's a bet, then?"

"It is," Kassidy said, her voice only trembling slightly as she turned her attention back to the older man.

Wyatt rested his hand on her thigh, smiling at Waverly. "Now I have even more of a reason to kick Brady's ass. My girl can't lose her bet."

Waverly laughed. "Oh, but she will."

"Doubtful," Kass supplied, side-eyeing him.

It wasn't until he replayed his words that he realized why. He'd called her *his girl*. Shiiiiit. "I mean, no one likes to lose, right?"

"Right," she said softly.

The table fell silent, and all Wyatt could think about was how he'd called Kassidy *his girl*.

Thing was, he wasn't panicking over it. If anything, it was...right.

What. The. Fuck?

"Dessert, anyone?" Waverly asked.

"Absolutely," Kassidy said.

At the same time, Wyatt replied, "No."

They glanced at one another.

"No?" Kassidy asked, looking at him like he'd stabbed a baby. "But I *love* dessert."

He choked on a laugh. "Well, then, we'll have it."

"Honestly. Who says *no* to dessert?" She shook her head, letting out a disappointed sigh as she set her wineglass down. "I'm going to have to rethink this whole friendship thing we have going on. I don't think I can make this work."

Waverly laughed. "I think you do, too. I'll have you know," he leaned across the table, smirking. "I *never* say no to dessert."

Even at sixty, Waverly was a successful, wealthy, witty, attractive man. And the way Kassidy smiled at him...yeah. It kind of made him want to punch the man right in his older, successful, attractive face. He growled under his breath.

The waiter came up. "Would anyone care for dessert?"

"Yes." Wyatt spoke before anyone else could. "We would like a sampling of everything brought to the table. You can do that, right, Jerry?"

The waiter beamed. "Yes, Mr. Hamilton, sir. We can certainly do that for you."

He hurried off.

Wyatt grinned. "Excellent."

Waverly whistled through his teeth.

Turning back to Kassidy, he winked, slid his thumb higher up her thigh, and said, "Still rethinking that friendship?"

"Nope. We're cool." She stood up, smoothing the skirt of her dress. Her hand trembled slightly, and her cheeks were rosy. "If you gentlemen will excuse me for a moment?"

Both men stood.

Waverly bowed. "Of course."

"We won't eat it without you," Wyatt promised.

"Of course you won't." She winked at him like he'd done to her seconds before. "It's a long walk home, after all."

She'd insisted on driving. He'd grudgingly allowed her. Part of him was convinced she'd insisted on driving so she would stay sober and keep her guard up. He didn't blame her. She was messing with his head, so maybe he was messing with hers, too.

Hell, he'd called her *his girl*.

Clearly, he needed his wits about him.

"Touché."

Wyatt watched her go, her hips swinging with each step she took. The smile he'd forgotten he was wearing wore off when he saw at least three guys watching her as closely as he was. He tightened his fists and turned back to his old friend, stiffening when he saw him laughing. "What?"

"You've got it bad."

He stiffened even more and sat down. "I have no idea what you're talking about."

"Yes. You do." Waverly shook his head and sat, too. "You gotta keep this one around, Hamilton. Girls like her are one of a kind."

"I won't be keeping anything around. She's a person, not a possession." He lifted a shoulder. "Besides, it's not like that with us. We're just friends."

Waverly snorted. "Yeah. Sure you are."

"We are," he said, leaving it at that. Protesting more would only make Waverly think he was right, and he wasn't. He and Kass knew what they were, and that was all that mattered.

No one else needed to know or understand.

"So, then, you wouldn't mind if she was flirting with a guy while waiting for the restroom to open?" Waverly asked slowly.

Wyatt snorted. "Of course not."

"Good. Because she is."

He glanced over, and sure enough, she was chatting it up with a tall dude who probably never skipped a day in the gym his whole life. She laughed at something he said, playing with her glasses nervously and then turned toward Wyatt.

He cocked a brow.

She smiled at him.

He forced a smile back. It hurt.

"Yeah. You look thrilled," Waverly said pointedly.

"I don't have room in my heart for anything but the game. Nothing has changed in that regard." He glanced Kassidy's way again, but she was inside the restroom, and the man who'd been talking to her was alone. He sagged against the chair. "Nothing ever will."

Waverly rubbed his jaw, his old green eyes far too astute for Wyatt's liking. "A man can love the game and a woman at the same time."

"Not this man."

"If you say so," he said slowly. "What do you have against love, anyway?"

"Nothing. I love football. I love my team. I love my coaches. I love my family. Hell, I even love you most of the time," Wyatt said, sitting up straight. "I just don't need *that* kind of love in my life. I don't want it. Never had. I'm happier alone, and there's nothing wrong with being in love with being single, despite what everyone else in the world seems to think."

Waverly held his hands up in surrender. "I never said it was wrong."

"But...?" Wyatt supplied, sensing there was more. "Spit it out, old man. You've never been one to hold back on me before."

"But you seem to like this woman a lot, and she clearly likes you for some reason, so I'd hate to see you let her go because you were too scared to try to care about someone."

"I'm not scared," he said immediately. "I'm just not interested."

"When someone speaks to your soul, when you can't stop thinking about them, when they matter to you...you don't just let them go, son." Waverly shrugged. "You hang on tight, and you fight for what you have, and you sure as hell don't refuse to admit it's there."

"We don't have anything there besides a friendship we both respect and understand. There's nothing to fight for."

Waverly shook his head. "If you truly believe that, then you're even worse off than I thought. Admit that you like her. Admit that she makes you feel alive."

Wyatt said nothing.

Waverly lifted his brows.

He had no idea how long they sat like that, silently weighing one another, but eventually Kassidy came back, sat down, and said, "What did I miss?"

"Nothing," Wyatt said immediately, breaking eye contact with Waverly since the older man clearly wasn't going to back down. "We were just chatting about football."

"Yeah." Waverly smiled. "Football."

The conversation continued as Waverly and Kassidy went off on another tangent about last year's Super Bowl, and Wyatt found himself strangely reserved. There was something about what Waverly said, and how he'd said it, that had shaken Wyatt to his very core.

Did he care about Kassidy? Was there something to fight for? Did she bring him to life? He was beginning to question everything about himself and Kassidy's effect on him, and as a man who didn't second-guess anything, he didn't like that at all.

As if she sensed his distraction, she leaned in close at a lull in the conversation and whispered, "Are you okay?"

He jerked to attention. "Yeah, of course. Why wouldn't I be?"

"It's just…" She fidgeted with the napkin on her lap. He noticed her nail polish was chipped on her thumb, and there was something so very Kassidy—so endearing—about that little detail that his heart skipped a beat for no logical reason at all. "Ever since you called me your girl, you've been acting weird. I didn't think you meant it. It was said in fun. I'm well aware I'm not, and never will be, your girl."

Something about the way she said it didn't sit well in his stomach. But he forced a smile anyway. "I'm not worried about that."

"Then, what is it?"

"I just have a headache, that's all." He cleared his throat. "Hey, did you get that guy's number that you were talking to?"

"What guy?" she asked in confusion.

"The one at the bathroom that you were flirting with."

"I wasn't flirting," she said, frowning. "He was just talking to me."

"Flirting with you," he corrected. "Did you get his number?"

She shook her head, her forehead wrinkled. "Nah. I'm not interested."

"Why not?" he asked because he was a glutton for punishment.

"I dunno. I guess…he's just too muscly for me."

"Then what does that make me?" he asked, frowning. "Scrawny?"

"Just right," she supplied, eyeing his arms. "Some might even say perfect."

He choked on a laugh and glanced toward Waverly, who had become the quiet one. It wasn't until then that he realized why—he wasn't even there anymore.

"He went to the bathroom," Kassidy supplied.

"Oh. Right."

"So, we're cool?"

"Of course." He leaned in and wrapped his hand behind the back of her neck, pulling her in and resting his forehead on hers. Inhaling deeply, he greedily breathed in her scent. Every muscle in his body relaxed. "We're so cool we're the Arctic."

She laughed, resting her hands on his chest. "Good."

"Very good," he whispered.

Their lips touched sweetly, because he needed to kiss her again, and it was in that moment that he knew that Waverly was right. The way she knotted him up so imperfectly was something he'd never experienced before in his life. And, more than likely, he'd never find it again with anyone else.

Damn it.

Chapter Twelve

Someone knocked on Kassidy's door, and she hurried toward it, her heart racing like it always did when someone knocked. For three weeks, Wyatt had been coming up with reasons to stop by and help her with things, giving himself an excuse to ask for another favor from her. And for three weeks, she'd been telling him no favors were needed. That she enjoyed his company without them.

Yet…he insisted on doing it anyway.

He'd helped her paint her kitchen. Laughed with her as she continued to try to master yoga in her living room, and then kissed her until neither one of them were laughing about failed downward dogs anymore. He'd even had dinner catered for them at his place after she confessed to never having tried authentic Indian food, and died laughing when she drank a whole gallon of water afterward.

If she mentioned something she wanted to try, he was there, ready to help her. These past three weeks had been thrilling.

Life changing. Amazing. A dream come true.

Yet, with all of that, no matter how great it had been, or how many times he showed her new, exciting ways to live, there was no escaping the fact that this thing between them, this fling that was everything she'd ever dreamed of and more? It was exactly that. A *fling.*

Everyone knew that those didn't last forever.

She opened the door, and sure enough, he stood on her doorstep wearing a smile, a pair of sweats that hid *nothing* from her (*Praise Jesus*), and a tight black T-shirt. His hair was still damp from his after-practice shower, something she now knew he did every day at the facility because he hated being sweaty. He held up a six pack of her favorite beer, a DVD of *Titanic*, and said, "Today's the day I make you cry."

She groaned and stepped back, letting him inside. "I told you. I don't cry at movies."

"Only because you skip all the sad ones." He walked past her, paused to back up and kiss her, and then continued on. He headed into her living room, talking over his shoulder as he went. "If this doesn't make you cry, then I'll start to doubt that you're a human capable of real emotions at all."

Oh, she was capable of human emotions, all right.

She was falling for him more and more each day, despite the fact that he would never fall for her. That showed emotion. Two of them. One, she preferred not to name out loud. The other, she had no problem admitting: stupidity.

Wait. Was that an emotion?

Shutting the door, she sighed as she locked it. "I never should have told you that."

"Yeah, you should have," he said, coming up behind her and spinning her around in a circle. "You can't say you've lived if you haven't watched and cried over sad movies."

"Spoiler alert, the ship sinks," she said, her voice dry. Resting her hands on his chest, she locked eyes with him, and he legit took her breath right out of her lungs. There was something about the way he looked at her that pulled her closer to him, entangling her in his web, and she was helpless to stop him. "And most of them die."

"Ah, but you don't know *who*." He tapped her on the nose, practically hopping as he dragged her into the living room. "That's the fun part."

She smiled. She couldn't help it. His excitement was so catching and endearing. "The movie has been out for most of my life. Do you really think I don't know who dies?"

"*No*." His face fell. "Seriously?"

She felt bad for him, so she fibbed a bit and said, "Rose, right?"

"You'll have to see," he said, excited once more as he dragged her toward her couch. Bringing back his excitement was well worth any lie she told. "Come on."

She let him lead her. "Are you ready for the game Sunday? After your loss to New York, you guys really need to win."

"Yep." His smile faded. "Fucking Manning."

She patted his back. "You'll get him next time."

"Yeah." He cleared his throat. "Anyway, my studying was finished before I came over. Still, I'll watch our last game one more time before Sunday. I like to know my enemy well." He sat and tugged her down directly beside him. Reaching out, he grabbed a beer and handed it to her. The DVD case was open and empty. She hadn't even seen him put it in. "And my friends even better."

"I'll watch with you," she said, swallowing hard. She hated sad movies. They were designed to make you cry. Like, what the hell? Life was sad enough without making you care about someone on the screen and then killing them off, thank you very much. "I can help you take notes and—"

"No. You're watching a sad movie."

She sighed and took a drink of beer. "I don't *want* to."

"But it's something you don't do. The new Kassidy—"

"Likes football."

"And needs to watch the movie first. Then, if you want, football."

Well, that was something, at last. "When do you leave for the game?"

"Tomorrow at five."

She took another sip. "It's gonna be a tough one."

"Don't tell me you're not pulling for me." He leaned forward and turned the TV on, settling down with his arm around her shoulders. His Old Spice cologne teased her senses. She'd never be able to smell it again without thinking about him, and that was okay with her.

"I'm always betting on you."

It was true. Sad, but true.

"You and your brother make another wager?" he asked cautiously.

She laughed, not answering.

Groaning playfully, he started the movie. "Please tell me no singing telegrams were staked on the bet. That's too much pressure on me. I can't handle it."

"Hey!" She whacked him on the stomach. His abs hurt her knuckles. "You said you liked my singing."

He smirked. "I did, but mostly I liked that it brought you to my house. Does that count?"

"No."

Closing the distance between them, he cupped her cheek and grinned. "You're welcome to sing around me anytime, Kass. I'm thrilled Brett bought me that singing telegram, and you lost a bet, even if you bet against my team and got pissed at me for healing too fast." His blue eyes sparkled. "I'm happy you knocked on my door and broke my vase. I got so much more that day. I got a friend."

Something stabbed her in the chest, something she refused to examine closely. "So did I."

"Kass."

She licked her lips. "Yeah?"

"I…"

Music played on the TV, telling them the movie was starting, but neither of them broke eye contact. Who needed fiction when you had Wyatt Hamilton on your couch?

He swallowed hard, still staring at her like he was about to either break her heart or change her life. Maybe both. "When this is over, when we've moved on, I don't want to lose you."

"You won't," she said, her throat thick.

"I might. Chances are you're going to meet a guy who can give you everything you want. Everything you deserve. When you do, I won't stand in your way." He ran his thumb over her chin with what could only be described as wonder in his eyes. "But this man might stand in mine. He might not want you to hang out with a guy you used to have sex with."

There was that phantom pain in her chest again. "Are you…" She cleared her throat, trying to break through the thickness choking her. "Are you saying you're done? Is that what you're trying to tell me? If so, that's fine. We—"

"What? *No.*"

Relief hit her hard and fast.

"Wait. Are *you* done?"

She shook her head so fast she got whiplash. "No."

A smile curved up his lips, and he scooted closer. People on the television talked, but neither of them listened. "Are we being honest?"

"Aren't we always?" she said breathlessly.

"I like to think so, yes."

She rested her hand on his thigh. If someone had told her months ago that she would be comfortable enough with Wyatt Hamilton to actually touch his thigh while sitting on her couch with him, she would have laughed so hard she got the hiccups. If they had told her she would know what he looked like naked, she would never have stopped laughing.

Yet here she was, with her hand on his thigh, intimately familiar with every inch of his body, clothed or unclothed. "Then say what you need to say."

He opened his mouth, closed it, and sighed. "We should have stopped sleeping together weeks ago. That one night should have been just that. One night. It's all I ever do."

Seriously. Was something sharp stabbed into her heart? "Like I said, if you want to stop now—"

"I don't. That's the problem. That's always been the problem." He set his beer down on the table. She did the same, though she wasn't really sure why. "Every sensible part of my brain is telling me we're taking this too far, and someone is going to get hurt."

"Why would someone get hurt? We talked about what this is."

"Yeah, but the more time you spend with someone, the easier it is to forget expectations and rules." He pushed her hair off her face, tucking it behind her ear. The gesture was more intimate than anything else he did. Maybe because he did it without thought. He just noticed something in her way and took care of it. It was so natural. So familiar. So *right*. "You could make me want to forget, but I don't want to make you do the same. I don't want to hurt you."

"Then don't."

She closed the distance between them, kissing him, and he groaned. It was long and deep and masculine—and also somehow possessively dominant. He pulled her on top of him, and she straddled him, squeezing him between her thighs. He deepened the kiss, burying his hand in her hair, and secured his free one around her hip, gripping her tightly. As his mouth moved under hers, he thrust his hips, moving against her, making her entire body tense and crave even more.

She always wanted more of him.

Like he said, that was the problem.

Maybe he was right. Maybe they should have stopped weeks ago. Maybe they never should have taken that step that led them to where they were now. But they had. And she couldn't regret that, or anything that became of it, because with him, she was *happy*. Yes, that happiness was temporary, and yes it would go away. But not all happiness was meant to last forever.

That didn't make it any less meaningful.

Or any less real.

He broke the kiss off, breathing heavily. "I'm serious, Kass. I don't want to hurt you. Don't want to confuse things."

"I'm not confused." She shook her head, trying to kiss him again.

He avoided her mouth, tightening his hold on her. "What we have between us is special. I never want you to doubt that this means something to me. That you mean something to me. But…"

"It doesn't change anything. You still don't want to be with anyone." She forced a smile. The words didn't hurt, but the fact that he needed to say them again, after all this time, kind of did. "I promise. This is just fun for both of us. Just amazing sex. Nothing more."

For a second, she'd swear she'd…hurt him.

Like he didn't like hearing her say those words.

Maybe, though, she projected that onto him because deep down, she wanted it to be true. She wanted him to want more. But he never would. What she wanted and what was reality were not the same. No one understood that better than her. "Right. Sex."

He kissed her again, but there was a franticness behind it that called to her soul and made her, once again, think there was more than met the eye when it came to Wyatt Hamilton. But those suspicions were dangerous. There was nothing buried deep under his words.

What he said was what she got, and that was all there was to it.

To believe otherwise was foolish.

He broke off the kiss long enough to rip her shirt over her head, and then his lips were back on hers with a desperation that defied reason. He undid her bra and closed his hands over her breasts, rolling his fingers over the hard peaks. Her stomach tightened, and she moved against him, riding him through the fabric of the clothing that was still in the way. He yanked on her leggings, and she stood up, shimmying out of them effortlessly.

When they hit the floor, his eyes widened. Licking his lips, he reached out and ran his finger down her stomach, over her belly button, and between her thighs. "No underwear?"

"Not today. I like to keep you on your toes."

Growling, he yanked her back onto his lap, threaded his fingers through her hair, and tugged her down. He stopped just a breath away from their mouths touching. "Consider me a ballerina, then, because I've been on my toes since the second you walked into my life."

Sliding his hand between them to touch her, he kissed her again. As his fingers moved, he thrust against her, driving her over the edge of madness and back. Every stroke of his hand, every brush of his lips, drove her higher and higher until she forgot all about what she should or shouldn't be doing, and instead, she just let herself *feel*.

His fingers circled her, then touched her, and she moaned into his mouth, moving against him faster. Everything inside her tightened, heightened, and pulled until it all just kind of snapped, and pleasure rocked through her. As she floated through an orgasm, he yanked his sweats down, rolled on a condom, and thrust inside her.

She cried out, holding on to him tightly as she rode him.

Every drive, every movement he made, only made her body quicken even more with pleasure so perfectly perfect that it almost hurt. He moved inside her, his lips attached to hers, his hands moving her so she kept a rhythm guaranteed to make her come again. It was in that moment that she knew no matter what came of them, no matter how badly this ended, they were perfect together.

And that *terrified* her.

Chapter Thirteen

Wyatt hadn't seen Kassidy in six days.

That was six days too long.

In between game prep, the actual game day, and practice, things just hadn't lined up for them to be able to squeeze in some alone time. They'd texted, and FaceTimed, but it wasn't the same as having the living, breathing, beautifully alive version of the real thing in his arms.

Thanks to his late nights, combined with her busy days at the family flower shop, he didn't think they'd get any alone time today, either.

The longer he spent without her in his arms, the more he realized he'd come to count way too much on having her there. The weird thing was that instead of scaring him away, missing her only made him want to be with her even more.

This understanding they'd come to was a one of a kind arrangement, and he wasn't going to take it for granted. Or her. Whatever they had going on between them, whatever they wanted to call it, it had been too long since they'd actually done it.

Since time didn't seem to want to free up...

He'd *make* some.

Coming around the corner toward the flower shop, he stopped mid-step, his stomach twisting into a knot that threatened to revolt. Inside the store, Kassidy hugged a man he didn't recognize. He had a clear image of them through the big glass window out front. As they pulled away from one another, the dude tried to kiss her, and she dodged him so his lips landed on her cheek.

Undeterred, the man caught her hands and spoke earnestly, and she nodded, not meeting his eyes as he ran his thumbs over the backs of her knuckles.

That contact, his hands on hers, hit Wyatt in the gut like a full-force tackle from a two-hundred-and-fifty-pound man in full football gear. He stood there, unable to take his eyes off them.

He and Kassidy weren't a couple.

Weren't exclusive.

Had never *spoken* of being exclusive. They'd just met a few weeks ago.

And yet...he was jealous.

There was no other way to describe his roiling gut right now. They might not have ever said they were exclusive, but the thing was, he hadn't touched another woman since the night she came into his life, singing horribly off key. He hadn't even *thought* of touching another woman, even though the opportunity to do so had been there.

It was *always* there.

But he hadn't *wanted* to.

Yet here she was, holding some other guy's hands, and he wanted to crash through the door and Hulk-smash his damn face until he stopped acting like Kassidy was his world. Wyatt rolled his hands into fists at his sides, ready to help her if she needed it, but from the look of things...she seemed completely okay with this dickwad holding on to her.

Who the hell was he? Why was he at her shop at two o'clock in the afternoon? More importantly, why was she *letting* him touch her like that?

They talked for another couple of seconds, and then the other man hugged her again. She stood stiffly in his arms, not returning the hug, but not exactly pushing the guy away, either. When it became clear that he was about to leave, Wyatt stepped back around the corner, waiting.

The door opened and shut, and footsteps headed the other way. Wyatt pulled his baseball cap lower as crowds passed, keeping his head ducked so no one would recognize him. Normally he loved fans and pictures, but today he wanted nothing more than to know who that guy was, and why he'd been touching his woman.

His. Fucking. Woman.

Shit.

Did he want her to be his girl? Was that something he was willing to do? Hell, was *she*? Shaking his head at himself, he walked around the corner again and opened the door to her shop. She glanced up, tension pinching the corners of her lips.

When she saw him, she visibly relaxed, shoved the note she'd been reading aside, and came around the counter. "Hey!"

He forced a smile, opening his arms to her. "Hey, yourself."

"This is a pleasant surprise." She slid into his arms and hugged him, burying her face into his shoulder and breathing deeply. Was it just him, or did she relax the second his arms slid around her? Yeah. It was probably just him. "What's up?" she asked.

"Nothing much." He kissed the top of her head. She smelled like flowers and Kassidy. He never wanted to let go, because as long as he held her, she would never hug other men who might be better for her than he was. "I missed you, so I figured I'd stop by and spend a few minutes with you before my practice."

She snuggled even closer, her glasses digging into his chest and her body loosening. "Hmm. I'm glad you did. I have the place to myself, so no one will bother us."

"Do you have time for lunch now?" He lifted the bag he carried. He was dying to ask who the guy was who had been with her earlier, but if she didn't want to mention it, then he had no right to demand answers from her, so he kept his mouth shut. "I brought Panera."

"I always have time for lunch with you." She walked to the front, locked the door, and flipped the sign to closed. Turning back to face him, she smiled. "Let's go in my office."

He swallowed hard. *Who was that man who was just here?* "Sounds good."

"How's your day going?" she asked.

"Good." He tightened his grip on the bag as he trailed behind her, watching the swing of her hips. "Yours? Anything fun or exciting? Do anything life-changing today?"

Like go on a date with a guy who wasn't unwilling to commit himself to you?

"Uh..." She laughed uneasily. "Nope, not really. Just working."

Clearly, then, she didn't want to tell him about her visitor. *Why not?*

If she was seeing another dude, she had every right to do so. He'd told her time and again that he didn't want anything serious, so if she decided to try to find something with someone else, then he certainly couldn't blame her for it.

If she wasn't mentioning this other guy, did that mean she hadn't found something special? Were they just messing around, like he and Kassidy were? If so, why bother?

She already had *one* uncommitted man at her side.

Why have *two*?

"Same." They went into her office, and he glanced around, absorbing every piece of herself that she'd put into this small, square room. There were fresh flowers on her desk. A framed picture of herself, her parents, and her brother. A decorative piece that held spare ponytail holders and an extra pair of glasses. There was even a Saviors poster on the wall.

She closed the door to her office and leaned against it, crossing her arms. "You okay?"

"Yeah. Why wouldn't I be?"

She tipped her head to the side. "You just seem…upset or something."

"No." He forced a smile and turned away, glancing in the bag. "You mentioned wanting to try their mac and cheese in a bread bowl."

He felt her approach. That's right. *Felt.* "Let me guess. That's what you got me?"

"Yep." He handed her the food. "I also got a turkey and cheese sandwich in case you don't like it, though. Tomatoes, lettuce, light mayo, no onion. Chocolate chip cookie as the side. We can switch if need be."

She didn't move, just blinked. "You remembered my favorite sandwich order?"

"Of course I do," he said dismissively, sitting down on the chair that was in front of her desk. "I remember everything you tell me."

She still didn't move. "*Everything*?"

"Everything."

When she stood there without moving or talking, he gestured her toward her chair. "Don't you want to—?" He cut off because she set her food down, took his out of his hand, and put that on her desk, too. "What are you doing?"

"You're too good to me," she said, her voice a mere

whisper. Climbing onto his lap, she straddled him and cupped his cheeks with her tiny hands. "When this is over, and the only time I ever see you is on TV on Sundays, I will still smile, because this time with you has been magical."

He swallowed hard because that sounded a hell of a lot like a good-bye. Maybe she had found that special something with that other dude after all. "You're the magical one."

She shook her head slowly, smiling sadly. "The fact that you think that makes you even more magical."

Before he could reply, she melded her lips to his, kissing him. There was something different about this kiss, something unspoken that scared the shit out of him. But at the same time, it drew him in deeper and made him want to reciprocate in kind. He also wanted to pull her closer and never let go. So, he did it.

But they both knew he'd let go.

He skimmed his hands up her thighs, over the sides of her hips, and across her ribs. Threading his fingers through her long blond hair, he closed his eyes and kissed her back with the same unspoken thing that hummed beneath the surface of her skin.

She stiffened for a second, then melted against him, rocking her hips and riding him through the fabric of their clothing. He moaned deep in his throat, deepening the kiss, and thrust up against her, hitting her exactly where she needed him most.

The whimper she let out did things to him—things her kiss had already begun to unravel.

If he wasn't careful, he'd let her pull him completely apart.

Hands shaking, she pulled his shirt over his head, breaking off lip contact only long enough to remove it. The second it hit the floor, she was on him again, skimming her fingers over his abs. Slowly, he slid his hand under her shirt and up over her ribs until he closed his palms over her breasts, teasing her until she made that sexy little sound that always drove him—

"Kassidy, where are those—?" The door hit the wall, and a man made a strangled sound. "Holy shit."

Kassidy let out a squeal and hopped off him, tugging her shirt down frantically.

"I'll kill you," Caleb growled, dropping whatever he'd been holding in his hands. "You're a dead man for touching my sister."

"*Caleb*!"

Wyatt didn't say a word. Hell, he got the whole overprotective brother thing. He'd written the book on it. When his little sister Anna had decided to sleep with the family best friend, a guy he'd actually grown up with, he'd been all too quick to kick Brett's ass. And Brett's intentions had been a hell of a lot more admirable than his own were.

He *deserved* an ass-kicking.

"Who the fuck is this guy?" Caleb stomped around the chair, hands fisted, and stopped the second he saw who was sitting shirtless in the chair. When he realized it was Wyatt, he froze, jaw hanging, hands still fisted, cheeks still flushed with anger. "What. The. Hell?"

Wyatt stood slowly, making sure not to make any quick motions. He might *deserve* an ass-kicking, but he didn't *want* one. He had a big game in a couple of days. "Hi, Caleb. We met before. Remember—?"

"Of course, I remember," Caleb snapped.

Wyatt held his hand out. "It's nice to—"

"No, it's not." He turned to Kassidy. "Really? Out of all the men in the country for you to mess around with, you had to ruin this one for me?"

Kassidy crossed her arms. "I didn't ruin anything."

"Yes, you did, because now when I see him, all I can

picture is him with his tongue in your mouth and his hand up your shirt." He dragged a hand through his hair. "Why didn't you tell me you were Wyatt Hamilton's girlfriend?"

She winced. "Because I'm not."

"What?" Caleb glanced at Wyatt. "What the hell does that mean?"

Wyatt swallowed hard. "We're just...friends."

"Friends." Caleb took a step closer. "Funny, I don't stick my tongue down my friends' throats. Maybe I'm doing it all wrong—"

Kassidy flushed. "*Caleb.*"

"So, let me get this straight. My sister isn't good enough for you. She's not good enough to be your girlfriend. Is that what you're telling me?"

Kassidy tugged him back, cheeks bright red. "Ignore him, Wyatt."

Wyatt didn't ignore him. "It's not like that."

"What's it like, then?" Caleb snarled, probably about two seconds from jumping at him with fists flying. He was shorter than Wyatt, and not very muscular, but he never underestimated an opponent...especially when angered.

"Don't answer him," Kassidy said, smacking her brother on the arm. "I'm a grown woman, and he's a free man, and we don't owe you *any* explanations."

Caleb said nothing, just flexed his jaw.

He didn't look any less angered.

"But I do." Wyatt cleared his throat. "I'm married to the game, man. It's as simple as that."

Kassidy let go of her brother and gave him a narrow-eyed glare. "*Wyatt.*"

Caleb said nothing. Just stood there.

Finally, he said, "You like her?"

Wyatt nodded.

"You respect her?"

Again, he nodded.

"Then what's the problem?"

"I'm sorry, man." Wyatt focused on Kassidy, whose eyes welled with tears. "I do like your sister, a lot, but I can't be with her like that. She understands. Nothing has changed between us to make her think otherwise." A weird hollow ache in his chest ripped through him where his heart should have been. "I'm sorry."

"There's nothing to be sorry for," she said, tears in her eyes but not spilling out of them.

Seeing those tears, the slight tremor of her lips, made his heart clench into a tight fist. "Kass—" Wyatt said, taking a step closer to her.

"Kassidy—" Caleb started at the same time.

"Don't even start talking to me in that tone of voice," she warned, pointing a shaking finger at her brother...or at him. He wasn't really sure which. "You know what? I'm leaving. I think I've had enough of one of you acting like me having a sex life is a bad thing, and the other acting like he did something wrong by touching me. Have fun feeling sorry for yourselves."

And then she stormed out.

It was a breathtaking exit.

Wyatt cursed under his breath and started to follow her, even though he wasn't sure what he was going to say if he managed to catch her.

Caleb put a hand on his chest. "Hamilton."

Wyatt stopped instantly, even though he could have easily pushed past the smaller man. "Yeah?"

"I don't like this, but I'm not stupid enough to think I have a say in what my sister does or doesn't do with her life," he said slowly, never breaking eye contact. He had the same blue eyes as Kassidy did, but they weren't as soft or warm. They hinted at a life lived fully, without regret, but also hinted that he'd seen some shit he wished he hadn't. "But if you hurt her—if you make her cry one tear that she wouldn't have cried without you in her life—I don't care who the hell you are, or how good your stats are. I'll fucking kill you."

Wyatt clenched his jaw. "Understood."

Chapter Fourteen

Today had been a disaster.

A complete, utter, embarrassing, awful *disaster.*

First, her ex had decided to stop in and make a passionate plea about how much he regretted walking away from her, and how he'd written her a note, and how she *had to read it*. She had. It hadn't changed her opinion about him being an asshole for leaving her. The only reason he was coming around again was because big-boobed Becky had left him.

So, he'd come running back to her, expecting her to be waiting for him.

She wasn't.

Then, as if that hadn't been bad enough, Caleb had crashed her and Wyatt's make-out session and probably scared her secret lover off for good. Why would he stick around for some "fun" with her after dealing with a stupidly overprotective brother who threatened to *kill* him?

It was over, and Caleb had been the impetus behind the ending, so she'd ignored every phone call, knock on the door, and text she'd gotten from him. She had nothing to say to anyone…

Except maybe Wyatt.

But *he* hadn't called or texted once.

It was well after midnight, and she'd been wallowing in self-pity and anger all day, but now that she was crawling into bed alone, she was losing the anger and going deeper into the self-pity party. Being with Wyatt had been incredible. Losing him? A little less so.

Still, it had been bound to happen eventually.

Might as well be now.

Rolling over, she sighed and checked her phone for the millionth time. There was still nothing from Wyatt. His silence spoke louder than any words could.

After putting it on do not disturb so she could sleep, she set it down, closed her eyes, and tried to shut off her mind. She'd almost succeeded when something hit her bedroom window, jerking her out of her almost slumber. "What the—?"

Something hit the glass again, and she stood, creeping toward it, heart racing. Slowly, hesitantly, she pushed the curtains back…and couldn't believe her eyes. She pushed the window open and called out, "Did you seriously throw *pebbles* at my window?"

"Yes. Did I wake you up?" Wyatt asked, still holding a pile of rocks in his hands.

"Yes," she said, wrapping her arms around herself. It was chilly outside.

"I'm not sorry."

She snorted. "What are you doing here?"

"We need to talk."

In other words, he'd come here to break it off officially. Regret had probably hit him, and he didn't want to upset her, so he'd come to tell her in person. "We don't, really."

"Yes, we do." He replaced the rocks he'd taken out of her flower bed and stepped back, craning his neck. "I'm always begging you to let me in your house, but that won't stop me from doing it again. Can I please come in, Kass?"

"I don't see the point." She rubbed the goose bumps off her arms. "I mean, if you're here to tell me we're done, I kind of already figured that out for myself, so there's nothing to say—"

"Kass."

She sucked in a breath. "What?"

"Let me in."

For a second, she didn't move.

Letting him in was a horrible idea. If she did that, there would be nothing to hold on to anymore. If she let him in, and he officially ended it like she figured he would, there would be no room left for hope anymore. Once he said the words, she'd only see him on TV from now on. She wasn't *ready* for that yet.

Then again, she didn't think she ever would be.

She closed the window and made her way downstairs. When she opened the door, he stood there, wearing his usual post-practice clothes. His face was shadowed, and he had bags under his eyes. The second they locked eyes, he closed the distance between them, pulled her into his arms, and hugged her. "I'm sorry."

She closed her eyes, enjoying his arms around her again. "There's nothing for you to be sorry for. If anything, I'm the one who should apologize."

"What? No." He pulled back, resting his hands on her shoulders. "I'm the one who said those terrible things."

She blinked. "You didn't—"

"Yes, I did. I said that nothing between us has changed." His grip on her shifted, and he ran his thumbs over the skin on her bare shoulders, slipping under the thin strap of her nightgown. "That's not true. That was a lie."

She swallowed hard, her heart skipping a couple of beats.

His eyes held a warmth inside them that threatened to set her on fire. "Wyatt..."

"I promised to never lie to you, and I broke that promise." He stepped closer, the toes of his sneakers touching her bare ones. "I think about you all the time, Kass. Even when I'm not with you. Your laugh. Your hair. Your touch. The way your eyes light up when I say something funny. And then I spend hours trying of think of something funny to say next time I see you so they light up again. You're always on my mind. Even when I sleep...I dream of you. In my mind, it's all Kassidy, all the time. I only have one channel."

She didn't say anything.

To be honest, she was incapable of speaking.

"I'm still not ready to slap a label on us, or to change the fact that football comes first in my life and always will..." He flexed his jaw, locking eyes with her again. "But things *have* changed. You changed me, and I think I've changed you, too."

She licked her lips. "You have."

"I'm sorry I'm an asshole who can't admit when someone in his life means something to him, but I'm trying to wrap my mind around the fact that, for the first time ever, football isn't the only thing on my mind."

And that right there?

Was more than she could ever have hoped for.

"I think about you a lot, too. When I'm awake. At work. In the shower. Brushing my teeth. In my head, it's all Wyatt, all the time." She lifted her chin. "I like you. A lot."

He rested his forehead on hers. "I like you a lot, too. I don't want to ruin this. Don't want to hurt you. But I also don't want to lead you on. Football is my life. It's always—"

"I'm aware of all this," she interrupted, brushing her lips against his. "I'm not asking for more than what you're already giving me. I've never asked for more from you, and I never will. I'm happy with you just the way you are."

"But you deserve more." He hesitated. "Maybe that other guy can give you more than I can."

She tipped her head to the side. "What other guy?"

"When I got to the flower shop, you were with someone. He was hugging you…and he kissed your cheek." He stepped back, rubbing his jaw. "I assume you're seeing him, too?"

Her jaw dropped. "No. God, *no*."

He continued as if he hadn't heard her, and started pacing. "The idea of another man touching you makes me want to kill someone. I've never been jealous before, but with you, I am. When he hugged you… I guess what I'm saying is, I'd like you to be exclusive with me while we figure this out. Unless you like him more. Unless he can offer you more than I—"

"*Wyatt.*"

He broke off, his cheeks red. "Yes?"

"I'm not seeing anyone else. I don't want to see anyone else."

He hesitated. "You don't?"

"Not even remotely." She tucked her hair behind her ear, her mind spinning a million miles a minute because, if she wasn't mistaken, Wyatt had just asked her to be his kind-of-sort-of-girlfriend. "That guy? He was my ex. The one I told you about. His girl left him, and he wants me back."

He stiffened, rage coloring his eyes a darker blue. "What? Are you kidding me?"

"Nope," she said, tongue in cheek.

Pointing a finger at her, he took a step closer. "If you even think about getting back with that pompous, vain, prissy asshole—"

"I don't want to," she said, smiling because she couldn't help it. Wyatt was *jealous*. She tiptoed her fingers over his chest and down his abs. They jerked under her touch. "But even if I did, there are things you could do to persuade me to stay with you instead…"

He backed her against the door, nostrils still flaring with jealousy. It was, hands down, the sexiest thing she'd ever seen. "Things, huh?"

"Yeah." She bit her lower lip. "Things."

"I've got things I can show you." He closed the distance between them, hauling her into his arms. She gasped and wrapped her arms and legs around his body. "But first…"

He nibbled her throat, and she arched her neck to allow him better access. "Yeah?" she asked breathlessly.

"I haven't been with anyone else since our first night together. I haven't *wanted* to be with anyone else, which is entirely new for me. I still have no clue what I'm doing, or if I can hang around for long…but do you want to be my girl? Do you want to make this thing we have between us exclusive?"

She pressed her palm to his stubbly cheek. "It's been exclusive from the start. Call it whatever you want, I'm here for it, and you. I'm not going anywhere."

"Neither am I." He smiled, looking more relieved than he should have been. He should have expected her answer would be an unhesitant *yes*. She'd been hooked on him since the first second they locked eyes. Heck, before then, even. "So, you're my woman…"

"And you're my man," she finished, unable to stop the smile from creeping over her face.

He grinned again. "God help us both."

Without another word, he pressed his mouth to hers and carried her up the stairs, ravaging her with each sweep of his tongue. It wasn't until he set her down on the tile floor that she realized where they were. The bathroom. She frowned, watching as he turned the shower on. "What are we doing in here?"

"I came straight here from practice without showering

because I needed to talk to you." He ripped his shirt off, his hard muscles flexing with each movement. His hard, toned, tan body had her full attention. She'd never get enough. "I'm gross and need to shower."

She smirked. "I assure you, I don't mind you dirtying me up a little bit."

"I'm sure you don't." He slid out of his sweats, no boxers on underneath. Just like that, he was naked in her bathroom. She'd never been so blessed. The urge to cross herself was strong. "But my girl only deserves the best."

Before she could wrap her mind around that sentence, he had her nightgown off, and they were under the hot spray of water. It washed over them both, and his mouth kept finding spots on her body to kiss. Her mouth. Her throat. Her breast. Her thigh. Her...

"*Wyatt*," she breathed, dropping her head back against the tile.

He spread her thighs farther apart, slipping his tongue deeper. She trembled, hanging on to his hair for dear life as he sent her soaring into the skies. By the time she came back down, he'd made her come twice. As he stood and prepared to shut the water off, she dropped to her knees. His lids were hooded, his lips parted. "Kass..."

"My turn."

He swallowed so hard she saw his Adam's apple bob. "Okay."

She flicked her tongue over the tip of his erection, smiling when he hissed and jumped. After lapping up the water on his flesh, she took him fully into her mouth. He groaned and pumped into her mouth, tugging on her hair as he moved erratically until she could taste his pleasure on her tongue, but he jerked away, breathing heavily, before she could make him come.

"I need you now," he said, his voice demanding and sexy.

Nodding, she immediately stood and hauled him close. "Yes. *Now.*"

"But I don't have a condom." He glanced over his shoulder. "We need to go to your room and—"

Too far. Too much. Besides, they were exclusive now... "I'm clean and on the pill. I've only ever been with one other guy, and I got tested after we split years ago. You?"

"I've been with more, but never without protection, and I get tested regularly." He hesitated, running his hand down her arm to entwine fingers with her. "But are you sure?"

She nodded. "I never miss a pill. I swear it." He still wasn't convinced. "But if you'd rather wait and dry off—"

He backed her into the water again, lifting her and sliding between her legs, and kissed her as he drove inside her with nothing between them for the first time ever. They both groaned when he buried his body inside hers. It was magical. Perfect. Amazing.

She loved him.

He might not love her, and he might never, but for now, he was hers, and that would have to be enough. She'd promised not to ask for more, and she didn't intend to break that promise.

"Kass..." He paused a second, pulling back with wonder in his eyes, and for a second she had the horrifying thought that she had spoken out loud.

No.

Before she could say anything or find out if she had, he swallowed her words with his mouth and plunged inside her mercilessly, driving her higher and higher with each thrust until she was sure she would die and go to heaven.

As long as he was there with her, she didn't even care.

He rubbed his thumb against her, sweeping circles that drove her crazy with need, making her even more wild. When she came again, he was right there with her, holding her the whole time.

They finished showering, rinsing off any remnants of their lovemaking, and afterward, he curled up behind her in her bed, both of them gloriously naked.

As he kissed her shoulder and whispered good night, she smiled, letting her eyes drift shut, and knew, at this moment...

Life just couldn't get any better than this.

Chapter Fifteen

The sun shone down on their heads as they made their way down Chestnut Street hand in hand. Every once in a while, he ran his thumb over the back of her hand, and she smiled at him, and to be honest, it was the simplest pleasure he'd ever experienced. Holding her. Touching her.

Having her.

It had been two weeks since they'd talked about being exclusive, and over a month since they'd decided to be together, and it had been a pretty incredible one. They'd spent as much time together as possible, and she never once seemed irritated with him if he had to practice late or watch some old games for prep, or if he changed his mind about hanging out in favor of spending some extra hours at the gym for conditioning with his trainer.

Football players usually had girls who complained if they spent too much time at the gym, or prepping for games, but Kassidy had yet to do so. If anything, she encouraged his focus. She even game-prepped with him and made sure he always ate well the night before a game and went to bed early with plenty of hydration.

Better yet? His game hadn't suffered.

He was able to focus on football *and* her.

Guess it was time to admit he was wrong.

He could juggle more than one thing at a time.

Smiling, he glanced at her. She sipped her smoothie. She hadn't been feeling well and was a little pale around the edges, but the strawberry smoothie was bringing some color back to her cheeks. This morning she'd gotten sick, and he'd held her hair back as she vomited. It sounded gross, and it was, but with Kassidy, he somehow managed to not care.

If she needed him, he was there.

Simple as that.

"Better?" he asked, squeezing her hand gently.

"A little," she admitted, averting her face. "Kind of."

"It was probably that sushi from last night. I've never been a big fan, but you hadn't tried it, so…" He shrugged. "At least we can cross that off your list of things to try."

She laughed feebly. "Yeah, we can." Wincing, she pressed a hand to her stomach, losing some of that color that had just returned. "Permanently."

"Are you up to watching some old clips of games? We can lay on the couch, and I'll rub your back. Maybe you can take a nap?" He lifted his mango smoothie to his mouth and took a sip. "I have to prep for Sunday, but if you'd rather me go home to do it so you can rest alone, I can."

She took another small sip, not meeting his eyes. "Yeah. Sure. Lying down on the couch sounds good. I don't want you to go." Swallowing, she glanced at him, turned away, and then back. "Wyatt, we need to talk. I think—"

"Shit," he muttered, stepping in front of her and releasing her hand immediately. The last thing she needed right now was a picture of them holding hands blasted all over the media, and the attention on her personal life that would bring. "Hello, everyone. How are you?"

She craned her neck to peer around his arm. When she spotted the group of photographers in front of him, she stiffened. "What's going—? *Oh*."

"Can we get a picture of you and your girl?" One asked, lifting his camera.

Judging from the fact that she'd been puking all morning, he could only suspect she didn't want her picture plastered over every Atlanta newspaper. When she went public as his girl, she would probably prefer it to not be while barfing.

He studied her, waiting to see if she stepped forward into the spotlight willingly, but she hid behind him even more, shuddering slightly. He took that as his cue that he was right. "She's not my girl, just a friend. And she doesn't need her picture plastered all over the media. But I'll pose alone and let you guys ask a few questions if you'd like."

Kassidy stepped back, resting a shoulder against the building next to them. He looked over his shoulder at her. "Do you mind?" he asked quietly.

"Of course not," she said, offering him a small smile.

She was pale and was pinching her lips together, though.

Shit. Was she gonna blow again?

"Okay, let's do this," he said to the photographers. "But make it quick, please. My friend isn't doing too well this morning, and we need to get her home."

A woman from the *Atlanta Almanac* smiled and lifted her camera. "Too much partying last night?"

"Bad sushi," he said. He posed, lifting his smoothie and smiling. After they all got their shot, he nodded. "All right. One question each."

"Where'd you eat last night?" the woman shot out immediately.

"Diro's."

A reporter from *The Sun* called out, "What's your

friend's name?"

"Not answering that one, but nice try."

The guy laughed. "Fine. Are you ready for Sunday's game?"

"I was born ready," he said, winking.

Another woman stepped forward. He wasn't sure what newspaper or channel she was from. "I read that you went to visit a sick child in the hospital last week. Is that true?"

"Yes. Daniel. He's a huge fan, and he's fighting cancer. I'm going back again next week to watch a game with him. I have every faith he'll pull through this." His heart ached for the ten-year-old. The kid was adorable, and a fighter. "I have every intention of visiting him as much as possible, during and after his treatment. If that's all—?"

"One more, please," that same reporter said, glancing at Kassidy and smiling before turning back to Wyatt. "You seem to like this child. Have you ever considered bringing another little Wyatt Hamilton into the world to grace the football field for generations to come?"

He laughed. "No. I'm sorry to say that there will be no little Wyatts running around. I've never wanted children, and I don't expect that will change anytime soon."

After a few more quick questions, he stepped back, checking on Kassidy again. She was even paler than before. "Are you okay?" he asked her, his voice low.

She nodded, not speaking and not meeting his eyes.

Turning back to the crowd, he pasted a smile on again. "Okay. We have to go now," he said, resting a hand on her lower back. "Thanks, everyone. See you after the game."

He led her away from the paparazzi. As soon as they rounded the corner, he said, "I'm sorry. I tried to make it fast, but—"

"It's fine. I don't mind," she said, her voice strangled.

Even though she said she was fine and didn't mind, he

couldn't help but think something was off. He replayed everything that had happened, trying to think of what could have upset her. All he'd said was that—*oh shit*. "I didn't mean it when I said you were just a friend. I figured you didn't feel well and weren't in the mood to—"

"*Wyatt.*" She let go of his hand and unlocked her door. After opening it, she faced him again. "I'm not upset about that, okay?"

"But you're upset about *something*," he said, walking past her and into the house. Once she was inside, he shut and locked the door. "I have a sister. I can tell when a woman is upset with me, and I know better than to ignore it when she is. If it's not that, then what is it? What did I do?"

"It's just…" She pressed her lips together. "It's nothing."

"Kass." He closed the distance between them and caught her hands, lifting them to his mouth. He kissed each one, locking eyes with her. Her green-flecked blue eyes were dimmer than they were last night, and she had bags under her eyes from missing sleep, but she was still the prettiest woman that he'd ever seen, inside and out, sick or not. "Talk to me. Tell me what's up. You can tell me anything, and I'll be right here, helping you figure out why you're upset and how to fix it."

"I know." She grabbed his wrists, biting down on her lip. "I…we need to…" Before she could get another word out, she clasped a hand over her mouth, eyes wide, and ran off to the bathroom. She was nothing more than a blur of blond hair and blue sundress.

He started to follow her, but she shut and locked the door before he could join her. He stood there for a second, hovering outside helplessly. He could hear her through the door, and it hurt his heart that she was suffering like this. He had half a mind to call the restaurant and rip them a new one for making his girl sick.

Swallowing hard, he pushed off the wall and went into the kitchen, grabbing her empty smoothie cup as he went. If history repeated itself, she'd want a glass of water after she was finished, and then maybe a cracker or two. He had no clue what the hell had been in that sushi last night, but it was pretty toxic.

He wouldn't be eating there ever again, *that was for sure.*

Grabbing a cup out of the cabinet, he filled it up with water, then set it down. After wetting a paper towel, he headed for the bathroom. He was halfway out of the kitchen when he saw the empty smoothie cup. "Shit."

Setting the other items down, he picked it up and walked to the trash, stepping on the pedal that lifted the lid. As he dropped the cup inside, his eyes caught the edge of a box that was tucked under a plastic bag, and when he read the words on it...his stomach dropped like a bad fifty-yard pass.

He fisted his hands, staring at the pink and white box, the world spinning around him.

He'd changed a lot for Kassidy.

Given a lot of allowances.

Taken risks.

But this...?

No. *Hell no.*

He was a quarterback. A free man. A guy who knew what he wanted out of life. And it wasn't this. It wasn't supposed to be *this.*

And yet...

He couldn't deny the slight flutter of excitement, underneath the shock, fear, and anger roiling around in his stomach.

The bathroom door opened from behind him, and Kassidy came out. "*Ugh.*"

He still didn't move. Just stood there, in front of the trash can. If this was real, what were they going to do? What would she *want* to do? How could they possibly—?

"Is this water for me?" she asked from behind him, her voice weak.

"Y-Yes," he managed to say.

"Thanks." She walked up to him, water in hand. "We need to…"

When she didn't finish the sentence, he took his foot off the pedal and turned to her, body stiff. So many emotions swirled within him, fighting for control. Anger. Pain. Denial. Fear. He grasped the anger that seemed to be the strongest thing besides fear, and firmly ignored that tiny bit of excitement that betrayed him by even *existing*. "Talk?"

She nodded.

"What the hell is going on?" he gritted out from between clenched teeth.

She bit her lip. So, she was nervous.

Good. So was he.

"I… You see… Uh…"

When she said nothing else, just stammered out a start a few times, he said, "Tell me that the pregnancy test box I see in the trash is just you being paranoid because you're late. Tell me it wasn't positive. Tell me it's your friend's, or your brother's girlfriend. Tell me it's bad sushi making your stomach upset, and not a *fucking baby*."

"I…" She paled even more, biting her lip harder.

He covered his face, his heartbeat echoing loudly in his head, and laughed. It was hoarse and not really a laugh, but hey, it was all he had in him. He should stop talking before he said something he regretted, turn around, and get the hell out of here, but he couldn't stop talking.

If he stopped, if he *thought* about it, it would be real.

Shit, this was real.

His heart pounded. His palms sweated. His stomach twisted into knots.

What are we going to do?

"Jesus Christ."

She made a small sound. "Wyatt…"

"Don't. Just…" He slashed a hand through the air. "Just give me a second."

She said nothing, giving him what he asked for—like always.

For some reason, that just pissed him off even more. She fidgeted with her glasses, something else she always did when she was upset or nervous. He knew that about her now.

He knew *lots* of things about her.

Closing his eyes, he cursed under his breath. Images played out in his mind. Standing on a field, the crowd cheering for him. At home as a kid, sitting on his father's lap in his library as he read a book to him. His mother hugging him tightly, singing a song to him and not letting go as her perfume washed over him. And last, but not least, Kassidy and him in the shower, discussing whether or not they still needed to use a condom.

Clearly, the answer was yes.

Also clearly, they'd messed up when they opted not to.

The question was…

What happened next?

"Say it," he rasped. "Say the words."

Tears filled her eyes, and she wrapped her arms around herself. Her lower lip trembled, and she stared at the floor as she said the words he swore he would never hear spoken to him.

"I'm pregnant."

Chapter Sixteen

Okay, he wasn't happy.

She didn't expect him to be.

Heck, she wasn't exactly happy, either. This wasn't her plan. This wasn't what she'd meant when she said she wanted to try new things, and live. She wasn't sure she even *liked* kids, let alone *wanted* them. But she'd had a few more hours than he had to come to terms with the fact that, despite her plans and uncertainty, this was a very real reality for her.

Maybe for him, too.

Though, judging from the fact that he had literally just told reporters he had never wanted children and never would, and the fact that he was about to break out in hives at the mere idea of his impending fatherhood, she didn't think he was going to step into the role so easily...

If at all.

"How did this happen?" he rasped, dragging a hand down his face.

"Well, when a man and a woman like one another, and they have—"

He scowled. "*Kassidy.*"

Okay, okay. Humor wasn't the right way to go about this, apparently. Fair enough. "I don't know. I've been taking my pill, and I didn't miss any."

"Are you sure?"

She crossed her arms, trembling with nerves that made her want to throw up again but trying to ignore them so she didn't mess everything up. "Of *course,* I'm sure."

He frowned at her, saying nothing.

"Do you honestly think I would lie to you about that? To, what, trap you into something?" she asked. Her chest ached as if he'd stabbed into it with a jagged knife.

Maybe that would have hurt less.

"I don't know," he snapped. "I don't know anything right now."

Ouch. Her heart twisted painfully in his fist. Despite his shock, she never would have thought he'd believe she would trap him into something like that. "I get that you're upset, but I'd never—"

"Upset doesn't even begin to scratch the surface of what's going on in my head right now." He paced in front of her, nibbling on his thumbnail. He bit his nails? "You just found out about this, right?"

"Y-Yes," she said slowly. "I bought the test last night on my way home from work and took it this morning after you got in the shower upstairs. I was planning on telling you when we got back to the house just now, but—"

"*Shit.*" He continued pacing. "This can't be happening to me."

"Well, to be fair, it's happening to me, too."

He said nothing, just paced, every motion dripping with his frustration.

Swallowing hard, she tried to speak again through the massive lump throbbing in her throat, choking her, cutting off her air supply. The room spun around them, blurring shapes together until nothing was recognizable except the pain racking her chest.

She'd planned a speech out in her head. Laid it all out perfectly.

But now that the time had come, the words she'd so carefully constructed in her mind were choking her, and she couldn't *speak*. "Like I was saying, you're upset, but I'm not asking for you to do anything."

He laughed. Short. Hard. "Are you serious—?"

"I stand by what I said," she interrupted, her heart beating so fast she swore it would take flight soon. "I will never ask you for more than you're willing to give me."

His nostrils flared. "If you're implying what I think...I'm not a deadbeat dad."

"I never said you were." She held her hands out in a silent plea. "And I'm certainly not trying to trap you in my life. I'm just saying you don't have to help me with handling this situation at all if you don't want to. If you want to walk away and act like you never heard the words I just said, you can do so, guilt free."

"Situation. Wait, so you want an...?" He hit the end of his invisible path and turned back, his face torn. "We'll have to take care of this ASAP. Before anyone follows us or finds out."

She cleared her throat, confused at his words. "No one will find out if you don't want them to. What you do, or do *not* do, is entirely up to you. I'm not asking you for anything."

"Don't be ridiculous," he said, stopping in front of her. "No matter what you choose, I'm here for you. I was just...it took me a second to get there with you, and to see what you were thinking."

Relief fluttered inside her. "Really?"

"Absolutely." He grabbed her hand and squeezed it, his eyes sad. "If that's what you want to do, then I'll take you to the clinic, somewhere private that the media won't find, and hold your hand—"

"Clinic?" She dropped her hands, her stomach sinking. "I'm not...*no.*"

He held his hands where they'd been moments before, entwined with hers, but now empty. "Wait. What? But you said you didn't need help with the situation, and that I can walk away."

"Yeah. You can walk away. But I'm not going to a clinic, and I'm not—" She pressed a hand protectively over her stomach as if that alone would keep the child she'd never even wanted or thought about having safe from the world. "I'm keeping this baby."

"Why would you do that?" he said, staring at her as if she lost her mind. "And why would you tell me I could walk away if you're planning on keeping it?"

Maybe she *had* lost her mind. "Because you can."

"Is that seriously what you think of me?" he asked, so quietly it hurt.

She hesitated. "I..."

Something closed off in his expression, and any hint of emotion he'd been showing faded into cold, hard anger. "You're right, of course. We aren't even a real couple," he said, his voice hard. "We were just fucking around."

She said nothing.

She couldn't. It hurt too much.

"And since we were just fucking around, I can just... what? Walk away from you and the child we created and never think twice about it, or you, ever again? Like we were nothing, right?"

She nodded once, pain blinding her. *Stabbing* her. "If that's what you want."

"If that's what I—" He cut himself off, his whole body vibrating with anger. "You're actually keeping this baby. For real."

She nodded again.

"Guess it isn't just about the fun sex anymore. So much for not asking me for more than I was willing to give, huh?"

Wow.

The way he said it, like they'd meant nothing, was that what he really thought of their time together?

He hesitated. "I mean—"

"You meant exactly what you said." She hugged herself, backing up a step. She needed the distance between them, to be honest. He'd put that initial wedge between them, and it was up to her to keep it there since he'd made his position on her news pretty clear.

Dragging his hands down his face, he didn't bother to argue with her. "I never wanted to be a father."

She swallowed hard, her throat unable to swell anymore without her breaking out into sobs. "Then don't be one. No one is making you."

"No one is—?" He took a step toward her, trembling with rage, his face red, nostrils flared, but pulled himself up short. "Do you *actually* think I'd *walk* away, and act like you weren't having my *child*? Leave you *alone*, without *support*?"

"I don't know. I don't know anything anymore," she shot back at him, using his own words against him.

He laughed. Actually laughed. "Unbelievable."

She didn't say anything.

There was nothing to say.

"This isn't happening. I've been so safe throughout my whole career. So careful to avoid this." He gestured at her stomach and then started pacing again, talking to himself more so than her. "And now, when I make one exception, in the blink of an eye, everything changes."

It was clear he was in panic mode, so she tried not to let his words bother her...but they *did*.

"I've seen this happen to so many guys," he muttered, shaking his head. "They swore they were safe. Swore there was no way they could have gotten their girl pregnant...and now I'm one of them. Trying to figure out how the hell—" He turned back to her, his eyes narrow. "Are you *sure* you took your pill every day?"

How could you be treating me like this? Biting her tongue to keep the words back until it hurt almost as much as her heart, she hugged herself. "Yes. This was an accident, a twist of fate. Nothing more. It happens. This happens."

"It's just..." He faded off, not meeting her eyes.

"What? You can tell me anything," she said, echoing his words from earlier.

She was trying not to get angry, to be understanding, but it was *really* hard.

"Is it definitely mine?" he asked, his voice so low she almost missed it.

She recoiled. "Excuse me?"

"I'm asking..." He locked eyes with her. "I've seen you with other men and even told you to go out and find someone else who could give you everything you wanted. I watched you flirt with other dudes, and we didn't even talk about being exclusive until two weeks ago."

Tears blurred her vision because he actually... "Wyatt, don't—"

"Have you had sex with anyone else since the first night we spent together?" he asked, his voice harder than she'd ever heard it.

"No," she bit out, clenching her teeth as anger overtook the pain inside her. "It's only you. It's only ever been you. Why are you asking me this?"

"Are you sure?" he asked again, his tone harder than before.

This was it. This was fully giving yourself to someone, only to have them turn around and crush you. She'd forgotten how painful that was, but now she remembered it all too well. This was why she'd become a hermit and closed herself off to the world. Because of this.

"Yes, I'm *sure*. I think I would remember having sex with another man besides you, don't you? Unless you think you're that interchangeable that I wouldn't notice?" she snapped, clutching the anger that washed over her because it was a heck of a lot safer than the pain still lurking beneath its surface, waiting to take over again.

He rubbed his jaw, not meeting her eyes. "It's just, lots of guys on my team got pegged as the father of someone's baby, and after years of paying child support, they find out it was all a lie to get money—"

"Are you accusing me of getting pregnant for money?" she spat, anger surging through her and chasing away the pain. Good. Anger was safer. More familiar.

"*No.* I'm just saying—"

She laughed, trembling for another reason now. "Get out."

"Kass—" he started, worry creasing his forehead.

"No." She walked to the front door and opened it. "Leave. *Now.*"

He didn't move. "It's a reasonable question to ask you."

"You're right—if I were asking for monetary support, it would be a reasonable question to ask. It would also be a reasonable request of a girl you don't know like you do me." She tightened her grip on the knob. "But I'm not asking for money, and you do know me."

"Do I?" he asked, flexing his jaw. "It's only been a month."

"You're right." She lifted her chin, fighting back the urge to cry. She refused to succumb to tears in front of him. He'd probably just think she was trying to manipulate him into staying. Apparently, when push came to shove, he thought she was that type of girl. "Come to think of it, maybe you don't know me at all. And I don't know you. Please leave."

He shook his head. "No. We're not done here."

"Oh, we're done."

He continued as if he hadn't heard her. "I'm just saying, realistically, it's not like we're married, or even a long-term couple, like most expectant parents. This isn't an ideal situation to bring a baby into."

Again. It hurt. His callous rejection of what they were.

But, really, had she expected anything less?

He'd been clear, all along, that he was a loner. She'd accepted that. That wouldn't change now. If he cooled off and realized later on that he wanted to be in his child's life, then so be it. But if he didn't, then that was okay, too.

Either way, she'd be fine.

Or so she kept telling herself.

"Ah, but I had a feeling you wouldn't want to stick around after I told you about the baby, so I guess I paid more attention than you, huh?" she said sadly, gripping the door as hard as she could. It was the only thing keeping her upright.

He came closer, stopping a few feet short of her. Just a few minutes ago, he wouldn't have stopped until she was in his arms, and that difference was as painful as it was clear. He was already distancing himself from her. "Tell me the truth. Why do you want to keep this baby?"

"Because it's *my* baby."

"It's my baby, too," he said hoarsely.

She lifted a shoulder. "If you want it to be."

"If you say that *one* more time..." He made an angry sound. "I never wanted kids—"

"Then get out. Get out and don't come back. Forget this ever happened. Forget me. I promise you'll never hear from us again." She gestured out the open door. "Despite what you threw at me earlier, I am *still* not asking you for anything you're not willing to give me. No one is making you stay, or even asking you to. So *go*."

He didn't move.

She lifted her chin, barely holding herself together at this point. "Don't make me ask you again."

"Don't do this, Kass."

His voice cracked on her name. That shouldn't have hit her as hard as it did, but it did. He reached out for her hand but stopped halfway, letting his arm fall back to his side. She choked on a sob, but she stubbornly held it back. He didn't even want to *touch* her anymore. "*I'm* not doing anything. *We* had sex. *We* did this. *I'm* just the one accepting responsibility for it, and that's fine, but don't act like *I'm* the bad guy here. *I'm* not. Neither are *you*. We just want different things."

"We can't do this. We're not ready."

"You're not." She lifted her chin even more. "I am."

He made a broken sound. "I can...I can try to—"

"No." She shook her head. "I told you I wouldn't ask you for more than you're willing to give me, and I stand by it."

"Kass..."

"Think about it. *Really* think about it. Do you want to be with me? Like, actually be with me? And this baby? Do you think we could be together forever? Can you give me promises you've never given anyone else? Can you be here for the rest of your life, at my side, loving me?"

He stared at her like he'd seen a ghost.

"That's what I thought. And that's okay. It's okay that you don't want that...but I do. I want more than you can offer me." She lifted her chin. "Good-bye, Wyatt. Please leave."

Growling under his breath, he stalked past her. As he turned around, mouth open to speak, she shut the door in his face because if she didn't, she'd lose it in front of him.

And she *refused* to lose it in front of him.

After locking the door, she stumbled to the steps and sat down, focusing blankly ahead. So. That settled it. She was doing this alone. That was fine. Everything was fine.

She was…she was…

Not fine.

Covering her face, she sobbed into her hands, pain twisting her heart into shards and making it hard to breathe. She knew, deep down, that she would be okay, and that she was strong enough to make it through this alone, and she'd be a kick-ass mom. This kid would get so much love from her that he or she would never even notice the lack of a father in their life.

There was no other option.

All this time, he'd been very clear that he wasn't sure he would be able to stick around, and she'd been okay with that. Even when he tried to warn her away, she'd refused to listen. Refused to back down when he told her he didn't want to hurt her. She'd decided the risk of a broken heart was worth the reward of being in Wyatt's arms.

And it could have been.

Why, then, was she crying on her stairs? It wasn't just because she was alone and pregnant and scared. She was all those things, but this was more than that. It was like she'd lost something huge. Something that she would never, ever get over. Like a big giant piece of herself had walked away. It was at that moment that it hit her…a big, giant piece of her *had* walked away.

Her *heart.*

She'd been an idiot and fallen in love with him, despite the many times he'd told her not to. She'd fallen for him, head over heels, and he'd walked away without glancing back. Maybe he'd return and tell her he wanted to be a part of her child's life. Maybe he wouldn't. But either way, what they'd had was over. She loved him, and he didn't love her. He never would.

He'd broken her heart like he said he would…

And she had only herself to blame.

Chapter Seventeen

Later that night, Wyatt glowered at the glass of whiskey in his hand, blinking at it, trying to clear his vision. It didn't help. He still saw two glasses, when he knew for a fact he'd only gotten one. Unless Brett or Chris had given him more...

Nah. Why would they give him *two* glasses?

Groaning, he set the glass down without drinking the rest. If he was seeing double, he'd obviously already had enough. Someone slid into the seat beside him, and he turned, expecting to see Brett or Chris, returned from wherever the hell they'd said they were going. For the life of him, he couldn't remember. Something about a girl, maybe...?

"Where did you—*oh*." Instead of his friend or his brother, it was a pretty blonde that reminded him of what he'd been drinking to forget: the fact that he'd screwed up with Kassidy.

She even had blue eyes like Kassidy.

For some reason, this made him think of their impending addition. Would their child have her blond hair, or his almost brown? A good throwing arm, or an uncanny knack for numbers and foreign languages? *Son of a bitch.*

He was having a *kid*.

There it was again. That small flare of excitement.

"Can I get a picture?" she asked, holding out her phone. Before he could say no, she snapped a pic of herself and him, then turned and kissed his cheek, quickly snapping another.

He blinked, trying to clear his mind. "Hey—"

"No pictures right now, please," Chris, his youngest brother, interjected, gently pulling the blonde away and using his firm cop voice. "Next time, okay?"

The blonde pouted. "Yeah. Sure."

She walked away, her fingers flying over her phone screen. More than likely, that photo of her kissing his cheek would be all over the internet before she reached her friends.

He was too damned drunk to care.

Chris sat beside him, shaking his head. "We leave you alone for one second..." His brother was every inch the protective cop right now, sitting on the stool with his back perfectly straight and his hand resting on his hip where his pistol usually was.

"Where'd you go?"

"Bathroom, like I said." He scanned the room, more than likely checking for more threats, and then turned his attention back to Wyatt. "Want me to delete the picture from her phone? You're pretty plastered, and she's probably posting it right now."

"I don't care," he muttered, dragging his hands down his face. "It doesn't matter."

Chris sighed. "Are you drunk enough to talk yet?"

"Yeah, we're kind of curious why you're drinking yourself under the table," Brett said, drily, from his left.

Wyatt turned toward him clumsily. He was engaged to Wyatt's baby sister, and they'd been friends most of their lives, but sometimes the guy was like a ninja. "When did you get back? I didn't hear you."

"The same time as Chris," he said slowly, cocking a brown brow.

"Oh." He groaned, rubbing his temples. "Shit. My head hurts."

"That'll happen when you drink the whole bottle," Chris said. When the bartender passed, he quietly asked, "Can he get some water, please?"

The bartender nodded and walked away.

Chris lifted a hand. "Cole's here."

Wyatt squinted across the bar. Cole was in the military and was rarely home, since he was usually off fighting for their freedom. Figured he was here to witness *this*. "Shit."

Cole came over, took one look at Wyatt, and snorted. "You weren't kidding. He looks like hell."

"That's why I called you," Chris muttered.

"You called him?" Wyatt said, frowning. "Why? He's got more important shit to worry about than me. He's supposed to be on leave, chilling, not taking care of me."

Cole clapped him on the back, grinning, and settled in on the stool next to Chris. "There's no other place I'd rather be than right here, with you guys. What's up?"

Wyatt shook his head. "Nothing."

"Bullshit. We're all here now. Time to start talking," Brett said, checking the time. "Spill your drunk guts."

"You guys are happy, right?" Wyatt asked slowly.

Chris raised his brows. "Happy?"

"About what?" Brett asked.

Clearly, they were confused.

"With Anna and Nina." He cleared his throat. "You're happy."

"Ridiculously so," Chris said, grinning. They'd been married for a little over a year or so, and as far as Wyatt could tell, they'd never fought in their lives.

He turned to Brett. He knew for a fact he and Anna got

into it a lot. They were both too stubborn to get along all the time. "And you?"

"I love her with all my heart."

Wyatt swallowed.

"But are you happier with her?"

"Of course," he said slowly, even more confused.

He glanced at Cole. "And you're happy single?"

"Uh…" Cole hesitated, glancing over his shoulder. "I mean, yes. I guess so."

"Why are you asking us this?" Chris asked slowly, his eyes wide. "Holy. Shit. Did you…did you meet a *girl*?"

He said that with as much shock as someone would say, *Did you kill a monkey in your sleep?* Like it was an impossible possibility. Wyatt didn't blame him one bit. All his adult life, he'd been professing his desire to remain single. He'd sworn to never fall.

And yet…

Here he was.

Fallen.

"No. No way," Brett said, laughing and shaking his head. "It's gotta be something else. Anything else. Did you lose your foreign sponsor?"

Cole lifted a brow. "You got a foreign deal?"

The sponsor Kassidy had helped him get? Even thinking her name made his chest tighten and his muscles ache to go to her house, knock on her door, and apologize for leaving. "No. I mean, no, I didn't lose the deal. And yes, I got one."

"Then…" Brett broke off, his jaw dropping. "Holy shit. It's actually a girl, isn't it?"

Wyatt ducked his head, not answering.

This was about *so* much more than just a girl.

They'd made a *person*.

A whole fucking person.

"*Yes*." Chris laughed, jumped off his stool, and clapped

Wyatt on the back. "I was right? You owe me twenty bucks, Brett."

Wyatt lifted his head, scowling. "Are you kidding me? You bet against me? Your own brother?"

"Yep," Chris said without a hint of shame. He held his hand out to Brett, wriggling it. "Who is she?"

Brett pulled a twenty out of his pocket and slammed the bill into Chris's hand. "She better be fantastic, since you made me lose to Chris *again*."

"I can't help it that I'm better at this shit than you are," his brother said, lifting a shoulder. "What's her name?"

Cole said nothing, just crossed his arms and waited.

Part of him wanted to lie and say there was no one and get Brett his money back. But the thing was…she wasn't no one. She was *the* one. The only one who could rip him apart and put him back together again. Since he needed to talk about it, and her, and the person they'd made, he couldn't think of anyone better to talk to than these three assholes at his side.

Sighing, he ruffled his hair and said, "Her name's Kassidy Thomas."

Brett cursed under his breath, probably still pissed off he'd lost the bet.

Chris shook his head, still grinning as he shoved the twenty into his pocket. "Cheerleader?"

"Model?" Cole interjected.

"Playboy bunny?" Brett suggested, grinning.

"No." Chris pointed. "She's probably an actress. A famous one."

"Florist shop accountant," Wyatt said, glancing at Brett. "You sent her to my house to do a singing telegram, actually. So, you only have yourself to blame for losing that twenty."

"*Shit*," Brett said, eyes wide. "So, this girl comes to your house, sings to you, and then you…what? Fell in love with her sweet voice?"

Wyatt choked on a laugh. "No. She isn't the best singer in the world—is quite possibly the worst, actually—and then she knocked my Hamilton vase over. As if that wasn't bad enough, she then yelled at me for winning the game the week before because she lost a bet. That bet was the reason she was singing at my house instead of her brother."

"Wait a second. You broke the vase Mom gave you?" Chris practically yelled.

Wyatt nodded. "Yep."

Cole whistled through his teeth. "She's gonna kill you…"

Wyatt winced. "Don't tell her."

"I won't." Cole shook his head.

"But—" Chris started.

"Focus," Brett snapped. "Enough about the stupid vase. Tell us more about the girl. You met her. She was awful at singing. She broke your mom's vase. And then…?"

Wyatt frowned down at the whiskey he hadn't drunk yet. "And then I asked her to go to dinner with my foreign sponsors with me because she spoke Chinese, and from that point on…I couldn't think of anyone else besides her. We weren't supposed to see each other again after that, but I went to her place again. And again. And again. I couldn't stop. Couldn't stay away. She was on my mind constantly, like a disease."

Brett snorted. "I hope you didn't tell her that."

"He did," Chris said. "That's why he's here drinking, instead of with her."

Cole snorted. "You're probably right."

"No, I'm drinking because I broke all my rules, fell for a girl—"

Brett choked. "Jesus."

Cole rolled his eyes. "Dramatic, much?"

Chris shook his head and took a sip of his beer.

"And then today, she told me she's pregnant."

Chris choked on his beer.

Brett's jaw hung open.

Cole lurched to his feet, eyes wide.

As Chris coughed, he slammed his beer down, covering his mouth and turning red in the face. Wyatt watched, slightly amused, but more annoyed than anything.

He deserved it.

Brett recovered first, dragging a hand down his face and saying, "Holy shit. Are you sure it's yours?"

"Yes," Wyatt gritted out, thinking about his earlier question to Kassidy. He'd hurt her when he asked her if she was sure the child was his...which he totally hadn't meant to do. He'd just been so *shocked.* "It's mine. I have no doubt. I never did."

"Mom's gonna freak the hell out," Chris finally rasped, pounding his chest.

Cole frowned. "Are you telling her? Or are you guys—?"

"She wants to keep the baby," Wyatt interrupted, seeing where Cole was going with his line of questioning. After all, he'd been in that exact same mind frame just a few hours earlier.

"What do *you* want to do?" Brett asked slowly.

"I have no clue. I didn't plan on her, or this, or..." He shook his head. "I'm clueless what to do, or what to say, but I was an asshole earlier, and she kicked me out of her place."

"And then you came here?" Chris asked.

"And then I came here," Wyatt echoed.

Brett shook his head, laughing slightly. "Shit, man."

"Do you love her?" Cole asked.

Did he?

What did love feel like? What did it mean? How would he recognize it?

Shit, he had no clue.

But he missed her, and he'd reacted horribly earlier and

needed to fix it as soon as possible… Not tonight, though. He wasn't drunk enough to think that knocking on her door and making drunken declarations to a pregnant woman would be a good idea. "I…have no idea."

"None?" Chris raised a brow.

"Are you sure?" Cole added.

Wyatt frowned.

"You said you think about her all the time?" Brett said.

"Yes."

"And you broke all your rules for her," Chris added, ruffling his brown hair with his left hand. His wedding band caught the light, reflecting it. Wyatt couldn't take his attention off that band.

He nodded. "Yep."

"Have you ever thought about leaving her? Never seeing her again?" Cole asked.

"Yes, lots," Wyatt admitted. "Especially in the beginning."

"But you didn't," Chris said.

"No. Clearly not."

"Why not?" Brett shot in.

"Because I didn't want to," Wyatt said, his tone dry. "Again, clearly."

"If she weren't pregnant, and you weren't panicking, would you be with her right now?" Cole asked, picking up his beer. Wyatt hadn't even seen him order one.

"Well, yeah, I guess. I was supposed to go to dinner with some guys from the team, but afterward—"

"Do you always want to be with her? Awake? Asleep?" Chris asked.

Wyatt hesitated.

"Would you give up anything for her? Do anything for her?" Brett added.

Again, he hesitated.

"If you can answer yes to any of these questions, you probably love her, dumbass." Chris shrugged. "Even if some of them are no, you might still love her."

Wyatt made a choking sound. "I don't...I just...I don't *know*."

"If you lost her, would you be okay?" Cole asked quietly. Considering his brother had been single for as long as Wyatt had, the oddly accurate question was out of character for him.

Wyatt swallowed.

Had he already lost her?

Was she done with him? Were they over? If so...would he be okay?

Never holding her in his arms again, and possibly seeing her in the grocery store with a man who would give her everything she deserved without panicking and running when she needed him most, made him ill. He wasn't okay with that.

And when he threw his baby into that image of her and another man in the grocery store, sitting in that little seat in the cart that he'd always found pointless and annoying...No. *Hell no.*

He didn't *want* to lose her.

He rubbed his jaw. "I don't want to lose her, but I might have done so already. When she told me... Well, saying that I didn't react well would pretty much be the biggest understatement of the century. I might have ruined everything today."

"Lots of people don't react well to surprising news," Brett said, standing. "It's how you *act*, not *react*, that matters. Actions speak louder than words, even when you're speaking to yourself."

He was right. They did. And his actions had, and always had, been screaming that he didn't want to let her go. Sure, he hadn't been planning on this, but neither had she. She was probably in as much shock as he was, but she'd handled it a hell of a lot better than he had. She'd handled the shock of pregnancy with grace and a strength he didn't possess, and probably never would.

She'd make an excellent mother.

And an even more excellent partner.

"Wow, that was deep, man," Cole said, lifting his beer to Brett.

Brett inclined his head and clinked his beer to Cole's. "Thanks."

Wyatt stood up, his heart pounding. "I'm not sure if I love her, or if I'd give up everything for her, but I don't want to lose her. I don't want this to be the end. And I want to be in my kid's life."

"Well, then…" Chris tossed money on the bar and stood. "What the hell are you going to do about it?"

Chapter Eighteen

It had been two days since she kicked Wyatt out of her house, and she hadn't seen him since. He'd tried. Oh, he'd tried. He'd been calling, texting, stopping by, knocking. You name it, he'd done it, but she needed time and space to clear her head. His reaction to her news hadn't been...*good*. He had all but told her she meant nothing to him, and that all they'd been doing was messing around. Call her crazy, but they were supposed to be more than that.

She'd given herself to him. Opened her heart after he told her she was more than a fling and that he wanted to give them a real chance at something. She'd let herself fall for him like a fool, and the second things had gotten rough, he'd bailed.

How could she trust him now?

If he came back around, begging for another chance, deep down she would always suspect he only came back because of the baby, and not because he wanted *her*.

She would never believe he wanted to be with her. Never believe he cared. Nothing would change that. He'd made his feelings for her, or lack thereof, *very* clear.

It was over. It was all over.

Her phone buzzed, and she glanced down at it, her stomach rolling. She pressed a hand to it, frowning at his name on the screen as she silently prayed not to throw up again. She flipped the phone over, not answering, and turned back to the reports on her computer screen. They wouldn't fill themselves out, and she wasn't emotionally prepared to deal with Wyatt.

He would just have to wait until she was ready.

And that was that.

When she'd seen the photos of him surface from the night they'd "broken up," she couldn't believe that he'd gone from her place to a bar with a bunch of women. She shouldn't have been—he never made a secret about his affinities—but he'd picked up chicks on the same day he found out she was pregnant with his child…so screw him.

The pain he'd given to her had helped her, in the end.

It had shown her it was time to move on…

Without him.

A knock sounded on her door, and she lifted her head. "Who is it?"

"Me," a muffled voice called back.

"Come in."

Her brother walked in. He wore a plaid shirt, a pair of khakis, and a baseball hat with the Saviors logo on it. He glanced around the room, seemingly to search for something, but his gaze landed on her without any hint of having found it. "Do you have a minute?"

"Sure."

He shut the door behind him, crossed his arms, and leaned back against it. He opened his mouth but didn't speak. After a moment, he sighed and pushed off the door, pacing in front of her. "I'm not sure how to say this. I just…you… well…"

"You're making me nervous."

"Sorry," he said, running his hand over the picture of the flower shop when it first opened years ago. "Mom and Dad have been together a long time. Happy. Married."

Kassidy swallowed. "Yeah...?"

"They love one another and support one another, and they've always given us a good example of what love is," he said, looking uncomfortable.

She said nothing, just waited for him to get to the point.

He would eventually.

"For a while, when you were seeing Wyatt, you had that look. That happy look. The same one they have in this picture." He pointed at their parents and then turned back to her. "You had a pep to your step, a glow to your eyes, or something corny like that, and you don't have it anymore. It's gone. I guess what I'm asking is...why?"

She swallowed. She'd never really thought her brother paid much attention to her moods, good or otherwise. Tears blurred her vision, but she blinked them away. She was a hormonal mess right now, which was another reason she'd been avoiding Wyatt. If he tried to win her back through soft words and softer promises, she wasn't sure she'd have the strength to do what she had to.

Wasn't sure she could say no.

"I'm fine, Caleb." She stood up, wrapping her arms around herself, and smiled. It hurt. "It's just...me and Wyatt didn't work out, is all. He wants different things than I do. We tried to make it work. To make it real. But..." She lifted her shoulder. "I want more."

"And you deserve it," he said, not meeting her eyes. He took his hat off, frowning down at it. "If he can't give it to you, if he can't love you, then he's an idiot."

"He's not. He made it very clear from the beginning that we weren't going to be forever, and I was okay with that. Even when he told me he wanted to try for more, I was okay."

Caleb frowned. "You guys tried for more?"

"We did. But it didn't work." She crossed the room, took his hat out of his hand, and set it back in place on his head. "You don't have to be mad at him or hate the Saviors because he's on the team. It's not his fault it didn't work out. If anything, it's mine. I want more than he can give me, even though he was clear he couldn't give it to me, so I'm the reason it ended."

Caleb frowned. "But—"

"No buts. I'm an adult, and I make my own decisions, good or bad, and no one else takes fault or blame for them. No one but me." She patted him on the shoulder. "And I'll be fine."

She didn't mention the baby.

No one needed to find out about that yet.

"If you're sure…" he said, hesitating and glanced over his shoulder at the closed door.

"I'm sure."

He grabbed the knob, not opening the door. "So, what should I do with him, then? Let him in?"

"Who?"

"Wyatt. He's here, in the store."

Her heart dropped, twisted, and sped up, all at the same time. "Oh no."

"Not so fine after all, huh?" Caleb asked, eyeing her.

"I am. It's just…" She closed her computer, grabbed her bag and her keys. "I'll talk to him on my way out. I'm going to break for lunch."

He glanced at his watch. "It's ten thirty in the morning."

"And I'm hungry," she said defensively. She couldn't see him in a closed-in room. There would be no escape. No, on her way out the door was the best way to do this. She would reassure him she was fine, get rid of him, and do her best to actually *be* fine. "I'll be back soon."

He watched her go through the door. "If you need me to get rid of him for you, or you want backup—"

"I don't." She stopped, turned around, and gave him a quick hug. He didn't hug her back. "But thanks."

After leaving her office, she took a deep breath and walked down the hall that led to the shop. As she neared the end, she saw him. She slowed her steps, greedily drinking in the sight of him. He wore a pair of warm-up pants, a hoodie, and a five o'clock shadow that killed her. His face was a little pale, and he looked tired, like he wasn't sleeping well.

He probably wasn't.

More than likely, he was probably too worried thinking he'd be stuck with her for the rest of his life, now that she was having his child. It was her job to make sure that didn't happen.

To not ask for more than he wanted to give.

She'd never wanted to trap him. She refused to. If he wanted to be a part of their child's life, then he could. But they were done...

No matter how much she wished otherwise.

She walked into the room, forcing a smile she didn't feel. He opened his mouth to talk, but she cut him off because Caleb was right behind her. "Hello. I was just on my way out, but we can talk as I go to my car, if you'd like."

He swallowed, nodding, his gaze sliding over her shoulder toward her brother, presumably. "Yeah. Sure."

She walked to the door, not waiting for him, but he rushed past her, opening it for her. As she walked through, he turned back to her brother. "I'll talk to you later about that game, okay?"

Caleb nodded, not speaking.

Wyatt let the door shut and reached out to touch her. "Kass—"

"Don't." When she lurched back, he dropped his hand to his sides. She'd hurt him, which made her a little guilty, but, hey, she was hurt, too. After all, he'd accused her of being a gold digger who lied about him being the father of her unborn child. "I think it's best if we keep our hands to ourselves when speaking, don't you?"

His jaw flexed. "Yeah. Sure. Whatever you want."

Part of her wanted to hate him. Part of her wanted to ignore that he looked so handsome standing there, staring at her like she actually mattered to him. She didn't. "I don't know why you came here, but you don't have to keep calling me, or texting me, or dropping by my house and my work. I'm okay."

"I didn't just come to check on you." He shifted on his feet. "I want to talk."

"We already talked." She hurried toward her car, her steps fast because she could smell him, and she hadn't realized how much she missed his scent until now. Her glasses slipped down her nose, so she shoved them back into place. "You don't need to worry about me. I'm a big girl."

"Can we talk?" he repeated.

"Talk. I'm listening." She hit the unlock button on her car, touching the frame of her glasses. "But honestly, I think we've said all there is to say, don't you?"

"But I don't mean—" He caught her wrist, pulling her hand down and trying to hold on to it, but she jerked free. "Sorry," he mumbled. "What I mean is, can we talk without you running away from me?"

She stopped at her car, facing him. "I'm not running. I just have things to do that don't involve you anymore."

"Like what?" His gaze dropped to her belly, then back up. "Is…is everything okay?"

Loneliness shone in those tormented blue eyes. His eyes shone with concern for her, and it would be so easy to misread that as more than it was. She'd already misread him once. She wouldn't be doing it twice. "Yes."

"Have you been to a doctor yet?" he asked, lowering his voice.

"No." She hugged herself. "I have my first appointment at ten tomorrow."

He nodded. "You're pale. Are you still getting sick all the time?"

"Yes, but I'm not pale." She shoved her hair out of her face when a gust of wind blew it in front of her eyes. "I'm just hungry, is all."

"I can take you to that place on Fifth and—"

"You don't have to," she said quickly. "I'm fine on my own."

"I can see that," he said slowly. "It's just…I'd like to talk to you, and maybe if we go out to eat, we can have some time together."

"I don't think that's a good idea," she said, tucking her hair behind her ear. "You were right the other day. What we had was supposed to be fun, and…and…not this. This isn't fun. It's not what you wanted."

"It's not what you wanted, either," he pointed out, shoving his hands in the pockets of his pants. "But maybe together we can find a way to make it work anyway. I owe it to you to—"

"You don't owe me anything," she said sharply.

He winced, stepping closer. "I'm sorry." He locked eyes with her, and what she saw there, the sincerity in his eyes, stabbed her right through the heart. "I didn't mean what I said the other day, and I didn't mean to hurt you. I just… I panicked, I guess."

"It's often when we panic that our true feelings come out," she managed to say through her throbbing throat. "But it's fine. We both knew what we were when we started. Just because I'm…because I'm pregnant…it doesn't change anything. You don't owe me anything, and I don't owe you anything, either. We're just two people, going about our lives separately."

He frowned, stepping closer. She backed up but hit her car. There was nowhere else to go besides in it. "That's not true. I didn't mean those things. We're more than sex. We weren't just fucking."

"Yes, we were," she said, tears stinging her eyes. "And now, we're not."

He made a broken sound. "*Kass—*"

"Don't. Don't look at me like that. It's not fair."

"Like what?" he asked.

"Like you care about me. You don't. And don't tell me you do." She reached blindly for the handle. "Just…leave me alone, okay? Stop calling. Stop texting. Stop feeling sorry for yourself and for me. I'm fine. I'll be fine. And I don't need you."

"Let me try again," he begged, reaching out for her hand. "Please, let me have another chance. I can't say where we'll end up, or what's gonna happen, but—"

"No. I can't do that anymore."

"I can try to be what you need," he said desperately. "If you give me a chance, I can try."

It would be so easy to say yes. To give him that chance, and pretend like she didn't see how it would end. But the thing was, she knew how it ended. He would walk away.

And she would be alone.

"I'll try to be everything that you deserve if you give me another chance." He caught her hand, holding on to it tightly before she could pull free. "I don't make promises I can't keep, but I promise I'll do my best to be the man you deserve. I promise I'll give you everything I have, even if it's not enough in the end, and I promise to try to do better than last time."

And trap him into something he never wanted?

No, thank you.

Part of her wanted to say yes so badly it almost took control of what little logic she had left, but the smarter, quieter part wouldn't let go. It would only hurt more in the end when they both remembered he didn't want to be with her after all. So why bother to try? He didn't love her. Didn't want to love her.

And that was that.

She lifted her chin, blinking rapidly because she refused to let him see her cry. "I want more. I want love. Happiness. Marriage. What we had was fun, but it's done. We're done. If you want to be a part of your child's life, I won't stop you... but I won't make you, either. It's your choice. Your call. You have nine months to figure that out. But as far as you and I go? I'm done."

He paled, stumbling back a step. "You're done."

"Yep."

"Kass—" he started, reaching for her.

"No. Don't *Kass* me. Don't touch me. Don't...just *don't*." She held her hands up, her lower lip trembling. She bit down on it mercilessly. "I understand why we're here. I'm not mad at you for not wanting to be a part of my life. You told me all along that you didn't want a relationship, that you didn't want forever. A baby is forever. I get it."

"But then I told you I wanted to try for more," he said calmly. "That I was willing to try."

"Right before you accused me of being a gold digger?" She snorted. "Yeah, I remember."

He winced. "I told you—"

"I remember what you told me. I remember all of it. Every word." She met his eyes. "But I didn't listen. I fell for you, Wyatt. I love you, so, no, I don't want you to *try*, and I don't want to wait and see what happens if we hope and wish you might decide to stick around and be a part of my life after all. I want someone who is going to need me as much as I need him, if not a little more. I want it all. All the things you don't want to give me."

He looked more shocked than when she'd told him she was pregnant.

Maybe even more scared, too.

That told her everything.

She slid into her car through the open door.

He finally snapped out of it. "What if I give you all those things?"

"You can't," she said, her voice harsh because she was through with these games. "Don't even try to convince yourself, or me, otherwise. I won't believe you."

He flexed his jaw. "Why not?"

"Because I get you, maybe even better than you get yourself. You don't want this. You don't want me." She closed the door most of the way, pausing before shutting it. "You're free to walk away and never come back if you want. I free you from all obligation. All commitment. All guilt. Be free. Play football. Have sex with random women all around the world. Kick ass. Win a Super Bowl. Whatever you want. You deserve it all, and more."

With that, she slammed the door, started the car, and pulled away from the curb.

As she drove away, she glanced in her mirror one last time, in case she never saw him in person again. She'd handed him a get out of jail free card, and if he took it, her child would grow up never being a part of Wyatt's life. Their child would never understand how Wyatt had changed her life, or the things he'd shown her. How happy he'd made her, even for a short time, and how he'd given her the greatest thing of all…

Before he'd walked away forever.

Chapter Nineteen

Cursing under his breath, he tossed another rock at her window, watching for any sign of movement from within. There was nothing, despite her car in the driveway, which told him she was home. When she hadn't answered his knock, he'd decided to try what had worked before, but even that was failing.

Clearly, she chose to ignore him.

This wasn't what he wanted.

It had never been what he wanted.

He didn't want to lose her.

Apparently, it took doing exactly that to realize what he'd been too stupid to see before. He might not be fully aware of what love was, or how it felt, and he might not be good at recognizing it when it hit him over the head, but if there was such a thing as romantic love in his world...

Then he *loved* Kassidy Thomas.

Why else would he be in so much pain because she said she was done with him? Why else would he want to curl up in a corner and cry, but decide to fight instead? Why else would he have lost a piece of himself when she told him she didn't want to be with him anymore, and that she loved him? It was because he needed her back. He had to show her he wasn't messing around this time.

That he wasn't giving up on them.

She *love*d him, and he loved her.

It had been six hours since he last spoke to her, and it had been six hours of pure and utter hell. He had a night workout at seven with his trainer to prepare for this weekend's game, so he'd decided to stop by on his way to try and talk to her... again.

Gritting his teeth, he threw his last pebble, not breaking eye contact with the window, as if his willpower to see her again would conjure her. It didn't. He closed his fists at his sides. Right now, he was a quarterback without a team. Without them, he was useless. Without *her*, he was a goner. Give him a playbook and a ball, and he knew exactly what to do.

But when it came to matters of the heart, he was out of his element.

His phone buzzed in his pocket, and he pulled it out, frowning, half expecting it to be Kassidy telling him to fuck off. He wouldn't blame her.

Instead, it was Eric, his older brother.

He'd gone and chased a girl across the country and was now living in Texas, so they didn't see each other much anymore. It had been at least a week since they'd last spoken, and Wyatt had told him about Kassidy. That had been before it all went to hell, though. Grimacing, he shifted the flowers he held to his left hand and answered. "Hello."

"Hey, man," Eric said, his voice loud and cheerful. Ever since falling in love with Shelby and moving to a small town in the middle of nowhere, he always sounded happy. Lucky son of a bitch. "How's things?"

"Not so great," Wyatt admitted. "If we're being honest."

Eric sighed, "What did you do?"

"Why do you assume it was me—?"

"What did you do?" Eric repeated, deadpan. "Last time we talked, you were into this girl, and talking about a future with her. What could have possibly—?"

"She's pregnant."

Silence. Dead silence.

"And I didn't react well."

A sigh. "What did you say?"

"I asked if it was actually mine—"

"Fair enough question," Eric said in his lawyer tone.

"And then told her about guys on my team who had girls lie about the paternity of their kids for some quick cash."

Eric groaned. "Shit."

"Yeah." Wyatt blinked at the flowers in his hand. He'd bought them at her store, and her brother had glowered at him the whole time. Clearly, he was no longer a fan. Again, he didn't blame him one little bit. He wasn't exactly a fan of himself right now either. "I messed up."

"Yeah, you did." Eric sighed again. "Good news is when people are in love with one another they tend to forgive a lot, so you might be able to fix this."

"She might not love me anymore," Wyatt admitted, his voice cracking.

"Do you love her?"

"I think so—" He cut himself off, clearing his throat. "I mean, yes, I do."

"Better," Eric said.

Wyatt turned back to her house again. He'd give anything to be inside there, holding her, telling her that everything would be okay. That he would never leave her. "How do I fix this?"

"Start with that."

"With what?" Wyatt asked, frowning.

"Tell her you love her."

Wyatt grimaced. "That's it? That's your big advice? Just tell her I love her, and it'll all be magically fixed?"

"You'd be surprised what those three little words can do." Eric chuckled. "But a grand gesture would help, too."

"A grand gesture," Wyatt said slowly, his brow wrinkled. "Like what?"

"Whatever you think will show her you love her, and that you're serious. For me, it was quitting my job and moving to Texas. For others, it's as simple as flowers and some pretty words. It depends on the girl and the guy and the situation, I guess."

Wyatt didn't say anything.

He was too busy absorbing this information.

Grand gesture. That's what he needed. The question was…what was grand enough? Quitting football for her? Losing a game for her? Winning one? Standing out here on her lawn until she accepted his apology and gave him another chance? Giving her flowers every day?

None of those seemed big enough.

Eric chuckled. "It's kind of funny. A year ago, you were the one giving me advice about Shel, and now here I am, returning the favor. It all comes around."

"Yeah, thanks, man." Wyatt swallowed. "I have to go. I'll tell you how it goes."

"Good luck," Eric said before hanging up.

Wyatt slipped his phone back into his pocket and set the flowers down on the stoop. Inside the bouquet was a note with three simple words.

I'm sorry.

—Wyatt

That wasn't enough. He needed his grand gesture. His brother had driven across the country for his. He had no clue what Brett and Chris had done to get their girls to forgive them. Walking up to the door, he pressed his face against it. "I screwed up, Kass. I know that. You know that. But I refuse to give up on us. You're everything I never knew I wanted, and if it takes me years to get you to believe me and give me a second chance, then I'll wait years."

Walking backward, still hoping she'd open the door, he moved toward his car. It didn't open. As he slid into his driver seat, he headed toward the gym, but as he turned down Walnut, he realized he had one more stop to make.

He knew what his grand gesture needed to be.

Pulling in front of the flower shop, he tightened his grip on the wheel. It was time to make this right, both with Kassidy and her brother. Her parents had no clue he even existed, as far as he knew, but if they were there, he'd make it right with them, too.

Clenching his jaw, he pushed out of the car and walked up to the shop, hands in his pockets. As he opened the door, Caleb lifted his head. When he saw who stood there, the smile he'd been wearing faded away, and he blinked. "You again?"

"Yeah." He hesitated. "I need your help."

Caleb crossed his arms. "I already told you her favorite flowers. I'm not going to give them to her for you, too."

"I gave them to her already. Or, actually, I left them on her doorstep." Wyatt ran a hand down his face. "She didn't open the door for me."

"Then maybe you should leave her alone," Caleb said. He came around from behind the counter. "She wants more than you can give her. It's time to accept that."

"What if I could give her everything she wanted?"

Caleb eyed him. "Then it would be up to her whether she wanted to take it or not."

"I love her," Wyatt said slowly, leveling with the man.

Caleb straightened his spine. "Go on."

"I hurt her, and you don't like me very much because of that, and neither does she. She might never forgive me, but at the very least, I want to tell her that she's my world, even if I'm not hers anymore. I want to make her happy, to never make her cry again, and I want to spend the rest of my life making her smile." He locked eyes with the other man. "But I need your help to do it."

Caleb was silent for so long that Wyatt thought for sure this was a lost cause, but finally he said, "What did you have in mind?"

Chapter Twenty

Not opening that door last night had been one of the hardest things she'd ever done. When he'd stood out there for a good half hour, trying to get her attention, that had been hard enough to ignore. Then when he said those perfect words through her door, begging her to give him another chance, she'd had to practically sit on her hands to keep them from opening that door for him.

Every other time he knocked, she'd let him in. Every other time he'd asked, she'd given him what he wanted. But not last night. Last night, she'd stood strong.

Being strong had never been so hard.

She blinked down at the forms she had to fill out, her eyes blurring with tears like they'd been doing nine times out of ten these past few days. It was maddening and frustrating, and she could only blame it on the baby, though, in all reality...it was because of Wyatt.

She'd loved him. She'd lost him. It hurt.

There was no denying it anymore.

Swallowing hard, she checked off the box that had her

relationship status as single, and then x-ed out the spot where she was supposed to enter her spouse's information. Nothing like forms at an OB/GYN office to really grind in just how alone in this you were. She lifted her head, glancing around the room to see if anyone else was as uncomfortable as she was.

A couple sat in the corner, holding hands and reading a *Parents* magazine. Another couple sat a few seats over from them, but the woman was on her phone, and the man stared blankly at the wall. In the other corner of the room was a young woman with her mother, both looking as unhappy to be there as she was.

She was the only one alone.

Guess she better get used to that.

Swallowing hard, she pressed a hand to her still flat stomach. *You won't be alone. I'll always be there for you, and I'll do my best to make sure you never lack for anything. I swear it.* With that silent promise, she picked up the pen again and started jotting down her address. She might not have Wyatt, but she had her family, herself and this baby and that was enough.

It *had* to be enough.

When she and Wyatt had first started seeing one another, she'd seen how this would end. She'd always stood a higher risk of falling than he did. Even when he confessed to wanting more from her than a fling, she'd known that eventually this would end with her alone and sad. She just hadn't expected to lose something bigger than herself when she lost him. She just didn't expect to fall this hard, and to be in this much pain.

She *missed* him so much that there was an unending emptiness inside her where he used to be. Every night that she slept alone, she relived what being in his arms, safe and cherished had been like. Every night she came home to an empty living room was a night she remembered how full it had been with him inside it, helping her cross another item off her list of things to do to truly live. He'd shown her so much. Given her so much.

Now she had to let him go.

She had to lose him.

Guess she'd have to get used to that, too.

Shaking her head at her morose thoughts, she returned her attention to the three-page form, finishing her address. The door opened behind her, and she heard a collective gasp. She didn't even look up. She had to finish this before they called her name—

"Is that Wyatt Hamilton?" the guy who'd been studying the wall whispered to his companion.

Kassidy stiffened.

No...he couldn't be here.

She hadn't told him her doctor's name. There were at least a hundred OB/GYNs in the city. For him to have narrowed it down to this one office, in such a short time...

"It is," the woman whispered, sitting up straight. "Why is he wearing a costume?"

Now she *knew* it couldn't be him.

And yet...

Slowly, so slowly she was half convinced this was all a dream, she stood up and turned around. When she saw him, she knew she was dreaming. He was in a 1950s costume from her shop, which Caleb had worn last week to deliver a singing telegram to a woman in her eighties.

A frigging *costume.*

He had on a pair of khakis, a button-up shirt, a bowtie, a top hat, and a pair of polka dot suspenders. In his hands, he had a seemingly endless number of *It's a Boy* and *It's a Girl* balloons, as well as plain pink and blue ones.

He locked eyes with her, his grip on the balloons tightening. "Hey."

"What are you doing here?" She pressed a hand to her stomach. "How did you find me?"

"I followed you." He took a step closer to her. "And I'm here because you wouldn't let me in last night, so I decided to come here to see you instead."

"In"—she gestured at him—"that?"

Wyatt smiled

It did nothing to hide his nerves.

He glanced around them, taking in the phones that were pointed his way. He was probably used to that. "It's all part of my grand gesture."

She blinked. "Grand—?"

"I've been told when a guy messes up, he has to make a grand gesture to apologize to the woman he—" He broke off, glancing at the phones again. No one lowered them. "So, basically, I'm here to make it up to you. Or, to try, anyway."

She hugged herself. He was about to say some pretty words that would make her want to forgive him, but she shouldn't. He didn't want this. Not really. "Wyatt—"

"I messed up, Kass." He took another step closer. She almost backed up, but instead, she stood her ground. "I never should have said those things. If I could go back and have a do-over, I'd take it. From the moment you knocked on my door and sang, I'd do it all differently."

She swallowed. "All of it?"

"All of it," he echoed.

"Why would you change that first day...besides my horrible singing?"

He smiled sadly. "It wasn't horrible. It changed my life."

"No, it was horrible," she said, the words barely making it out through her swollen throat. "We've gone over this before. I can't sing. It's no secret."

"But I have to tell you something," he said, shifting his weight. "I'm even worse."

Her eyes widened. "No."

"Yes. I can't carry a tune."

She choked on a laugh. "Liar."

"I'm not lying." He rolled his shoulders. "I promise, here and now, to never lie to you again. That every word I say to you, from here on out, will be the truth. And I don't make promises I can't keep, Kass. Do you believe me?"

"Yeah. Sure. Okay."

"If you don't, then I'll wait till you can. Until you do. I'm a patient man."

She snorted. "Not really."

"Well, I'll try to be," he admitted sheepishly. "Now. Where was I?"

"You said you'd have never opened the door that day," she supplied.

"That's not what I was saying."

The mother stood up, trying to get a better angle. She was probably on Facebook Live or something, showing the world what Wyatt Hamilton was up to at the OB/GYN.

She tried to ignore the audience, since he seemed to be doing so, but having people record their conversation was *weird*. "Then, what would you change?"

"On that first night, I would tell you that you intrigued me, and I'd tell you that for the first time in my life I was thinking about something more than myself and my career."

She swallowed. "Oh yeah?"

"Yeah." He took two more steps toward her. "That second time, I'd tell you that I came back because I couldn't stop thinking about you, and that I thought this thing I was feeling for you might be called infatuation." Another step. "By the third time, I would have admitted something I never thought I'd admit my whole life. I'd tell you I was falling for you, and that I was terrified of it all, but that I wasn't going to leave. That I *couldn't* leave."

Tears burned her eyes, and she sucked in a ragged breath, shaking her head. These were just words. Pretty words, but still. He didn't want this. "Don't say things you'll regret."

"I won't regret this. I regret a lot of things I said the other day, but not this. Not you." He pressed his mouth into a thin line. "Never you."

She didn't say anything.

Truth was she wasn't sure what to say.

"You don't believe me, and that's because I fu—messed up," he said, glancing at the cameras again. "Those things you talked about wanting? I want them, too."

She didn't move.

Didn't dare to breathe.

If this was a dream…she never wanted to wake up.

"Last time we were in public together, I denied that you were my girl. I told everyone you were a friend." He addressed their little crowd. "She's not a friend. She's more. She's the mother of my child, and I want to spend the rest of my life with her if she'll let me."

She gasped, covering her mouth, and dropped the clipboard to the floor.

"She doesn't believe I want this. She thinks I want to walk away from her and our unborn child, so…" He turned back to Kassidy, giving her his full attention again. "So, I'm going to do the most embarrassing thing I can think of to show you I'm not kidding around. That I want to be with you, and I'm in this for the long haul. Not for the maybes. Not for the casual. I want it all…with you. A relationship. Trust. Love. Marriage. I'm all in, babe. I never thought I'd say this to a woman, or that I'd feel this way about anything besides football and my family, but…I…I love you. I love you, Kass, and I don't want to lose you ever again."

She held her breath, tears rolling down her cheeks at those beautiful words coming out of his mouth, and shook her head because she knew what he was about to do, and it was going to be on *camera*. "You don't have to do this. I—"

"Yes, I do. We started out this way, and now we're going to take our fresh start, our new beginning, the same way. It's got to come full circle." His lips quirked into a half smile. "With a song."

Without breaking eye contact, he opened his mouth, and started singing "She's Having My Baby." He was right. He was awful. He couldn't hold a single note properly.

Still.

It was the most beautiful thing she'd ever heard.

Chapter Twenty-One

The more he sang, the more he realized he should never, ever do so again, but he didn't stop. He wouldn't stop until Kassidy realized he was the man she deserved. Until she knew, without a doubt, that he meant every word he said about wanting to be with her. Never again would she doubt his love for her, or the how happy she made him. Never again would he leave her.

She *had* to know that.

There was no hesitation left inside of him.

He'd had her. He'd lost her. He knew which side of the field had the better vantage point. If he had to choose between a life with her or without her, he'd choose with her every damn time.

His brother had asked him if he would do anything for her, give up anything for her, and he now knew the answer to that question. *Yes.* Unequivocally yes.

Hell, he'd even make a fool out of himself, with cameras rolling, knowing this video would show up on the news by this afternoon, and he didn't regret a second of it.

Not if it got him his girl back.

If it didn't? He'd find another way. And another. And another, until one of them worked. She'd told him she wanted a lifetime of forever with him, and even if it was the last thing he did, he'd give it to her.

He'd give her *everything*.

As he finished the last note, he caught her hand, holding on to the balloons tightly, and bowed, breathing heavier than when he sprinted down the field to escape an opponent.

The crowd cheered, and he grinned, bowing playfully to them as well.

Turning back to Kassidy, he slowly reached out to cup her cheek, giving her time to reject him if she chose to. She didn't. When he touched her skin for the first time in what felt like years, it was like all was well with the world again. He could be standing under an Earth-destroying asteroid heading straight for him, but as long as he had her skin touching his, he would be okay.

"That was *horrible*," she said, laughing with wet cheeks.

"You're crying, so it must have been," he joked, wiping her cheeks off. "Sorry. I didn't mean to ruin your makeup like that."

"That's not why I'm crying," she replied, playfully swatting his arm then grabbing on to him as if she never wanted to let go. "Wyatt..."

"I love you, Kassidy. I love you, and I'm never going to stop loving you. I've never put someone first or wanted someone's happiness even more than my own, but I get it now. I would do anything, give up anything, for you." He hesitated, then added, "I'll even walk away from football if that's what it takes for you to give me another chance. That's how much I love—*ow*!" She'd smacked his arm. "What the hell?"

The crowd around them went wild, talking about him quitting, but he ignored them.

All that mattered was what his girl wanted.

And what was best for his child.

His child… Fuck, he couldn't even wrap his mind around the fact that he and Kassidy had made a person. A child. Their child. They were a family, and he'd never let them down again.

"Listen, mister." She smacked him again, and he rubbed his arm. "If you *ever* talk about quitting football again, I'll kick your ass so hard you won't be able to sit for a *week*."

He held his hands up, laughing. "Okay, okay. I won't. I swear."

"Good." She grabbed his hands, and he dropped the balloons, letting them float up the few feet to the ceiling. "Are you sure you want this? I told you, I'll be fine on my own. I can—"

"*Kass.*"

She broke off, her cheeks flushing. "Yeah?"

"Shut up and kiss me."

A small laugh escaped her, and she rose on tiptoe, wrapping her arms around him as she pressed her mouth to his. The crowd around them went wild, and he smiled against her mouth as she laughed, hugging him even tighter. "I love you," he whispered.

"I love you, too," she breathed, kissing him again.

He pulled her against him, hugging her as tightly as he dared, and she let out a little squeak. He released his hold a little and pulled back, staring down into her bright blue eyes. "I hope he has your eyes, my arm, and your brain."

"She might have all those things, but she'd better have your dimples, too."

"And my arm," he added, still smiling like a fool. "Who says a girl can't play quarterback in the NFL?"

Kassidy rolled her eyes. "Society?"

"Not by the time we get done with it," he said, his voice

low. "Or her."

She smiled. "Is this real?"

"Oh, it's real." He touched her stomach. "You see, when two people love one another, and they have—"

She smacked him again, her cheeks going even redder. "*Wyatt.*"

"What?" he asked, his eyes wide and innocent.

"There are kids—"

"Ms. Thomas?" the nurse said, opening the door and glancing up from her clipboard. "And...Wyatt...Hamilton?" Her eyes were bigger than Kassidy's had been moments ago.

He bowed. "You missed the show."

"Apparently," she said. "Well, if it's over, and you're ready, your room is available."

Kassidy smiled. "Are you ready?"

"Oh, I'm definitely ready," Wyatt said, holding his hand out for hers.

She glanced at his hand, then took it, her fingers sliding perfectly into the spaces between his. Everything about them had been like that from day one.

It just *fit.*

Epilogue

The constant beeping of the machines had been annoyingly persistent at first, but now the sound was somehow oddly peaceful and soothing. The nightlight over her bed had been left on, but the rest of the room was darkened and quiet... except for the unfamiliar sounds of a crying baby. The second Marcus had woken up and made a sound, she'd snapped to attention.

She'd always been a heavy sleeper, and deep down she had worried she might not make a good mother because of that, but lo and behold. If her child so much as squeaked... she was there.

She sat up, blinking and gingerly raising herself to sit. She glanced into the little plastic bassinet thing all hospitals had, her heart racing when she saw it was empty. Her heart twisted painfully. "*Marcus.* Oh my—"

"Shh. It's okay." Wyatt came from a dark corner of the room, little Marcus in his arms. "I have him. We had a dirty diaper situation that needed attending to."

She collapsed against the back of the bed, breathing

heavily, pressing a hand to her racing heart. Clumsily, she shoved her glasses into place, blinking at him. "You scared the crap out of me. I thought you went home to shower and change."

"I did." He came closer, patting the baby's back as he approached, smiling. His titanium wedding band reflected the dim nightlight, making it shine for a moment. His hair was still damp from his shower, and he wore a pair of sweats and a Saviors shirt. "But did you honestly think I'd be able to stay away from two of my favorite people for longer than an hour?"

She smiled, despite her still racing heart. "Of course not. But there's not a bed for you."

"I don't need a bed." He sat on the chair beside her, resting his feet on the ottoman. "All I need is you and Marcus."

Gingerly, she reclined again, rolling onto her side and watching as her husband rocked their child to sleep. They'd had a low-key wedding, a justice-of-the-peace affair with family and a few friends. It had been intimate and private, and the magazines had been angry to miss it all.

Marcus's eyes closed, his little lips pursed perfectly as he sucked on nothing at all. He was so tiny. So perfect. So *theirs*. "He has your dimples."

"But your eyes." Wyatt leaned down to kiss the baby's forehead. He flailed, freeing himself from the swaddling, and punched Wyatt in the nose. Wyatt lurched back, blinking rapidly. "*Ow.*"

"And your arm," she said, laughing as he rubbed the bridge of his nose.

"Clearly," he said with pride. He locked eyes with her, smiling. "I love you."

"I love you, too," she whispered. "Why don't you sing him to sleep?"

"And give him nightmares?"

Kassidy laughed. "Fine. Then sing me to sleep."

Wyatt chuckled and whispered, "Rest, my love. I'll be here when you wake up. We'll both be here."

Kassidy let her lids drift shut. He was telling the truth. Everything hurt, and things were sore that she hadn't even known existed, but she'd never been more at peace with herself and life in general than she was right now, right here, in this private hospital room Wyatt had insisted they get. Funny, she remembered lying in bed with Wyatt, before she'd gotten pregnant, and thinking that there was no way life could get any better than that moment.

She'd been wrong.

It had gotten *so* much better.

Life. Was. Good.

About the Author

Diane Alberts is a multi-published, bestselling contemporary romance author with Entangled Publishing. She also writes *New York Times*, *USA Today*, and *Wall Street Journal* bestselling new adult books under the name Jen McLaughlin. She's hit the Top 100 lists on Amazon and Barnes and Noble numerous times with numerous titles. She was mentioned in Forbes alongside E. L. James as one of the breakout independent authors to dominate the bestselling lists. Diane is represented by Louise Fury at The Bent Agency.

.

Discover more category romance titles from Entangled Indulgence...

69 MILLION THINGS I HATE ABOUT YOU
a *Winning the Billionaire* novel by Kira Archer

After Kiersten wins sixty-nine million dollars in the lotto, she has more than enough money to quit working for her impossibly demanding boss. But where's the fun in that? When billionaire Cole Harrington finds out about the office pool betting on how long it'll take him to fire his usually agreeable assistant, he decides to spice things up and see how far he can push her until she quits. But the bet sparks a new dynamic between them, and they cross that fine line between hate and love.

TAKEN BY THE CEO
a *Scandalous Wentworths* novel by Stefanie London

When Emmaline Greene pretends to be confident, sexy Sarah, she figures no harm, no foul. Her one-night stand will never find out. *Wrong.* The gorgeous guy she slept with is new boss. Parker Wentworth has a lot to prove. He's just been appointed CEO of his family's company and is tasked with repairing its scandalous reputation. He can't afford any distractions or complications. Too bad the attractive blonde he takes to bed turns out to be both.

CPSIA information can be obtained
at www.ICGtesting.com
Printed in the USA
LVOW10s2259270218
568151LV00001B/20/P